T0146480

Through the Mirrorball

Books by Rob Browatzke

Wonderland

Through the Mirrorball

Published by Kensington Publishing Corporation

Through the Mirrorball

Rob Browatzke

LYRICAL PRESS
Kensington Publishing Corp.
www.kensingtonbooks.com

To the extent that the image or images on the cover of this book depict a person or persons, such person or persons are merely models, and are not intended to portray any character or characters featured in the book.

LYRICAL PRESS BOOKS are published by

Kensington Publishing Corp.
119 West 40th Street
New York, NY 10018

Copyright © 2015 by Rob Browatzke

All rights reserved. No part of this book may be reproduced in any form or by any means without the prior written consent of the Publisher, excepting brief quotes used in reviews.

All Kensington titles, imprints, and distributed lines are available at special quantity discounts for bulk purchases for sales promotion, premiums, fund-raising, educational, or institutional use.

Special book excerpts or customized printings can also be created to fit specific needs. For details, write or phone the office of the Kensington Sales Manager: Kensington Publishing Corp., 119 West 40th Street, New York, NY 10018. Attn. Sales Department. Phone: 1-800-221-2647.

Lyrical and the L logo are trademarks of Kensington Publishing Corp.

First Electronic Edition: May 2015
eISBN-13: 978-1-60183-370-9
eISBN-10: 1-60183-370-9

First Print Edition: May 2015
ISBN-13: 978-1-60183-371-6
ISBN-10: 1-60183-371-7

Printed in the United States of America

Alex wouldn't be here, having curiouser and curiouser adventures without the support of people like Kari, Murray, and Scott, and without the inspiration and exasperation of all the boys in our WonderLounge

Chapter 1

The morning after I rescued Steven was perhaps the best morning of my life. All the trauma, all the drama, of the past week was over, and it was just us again. Together. The way we belonged.

I woke up before him, and lay there in bed, watching him sleep. It had been such a hellish week, starting with that fight, and then him disappearing, all the calls tormenting me, and then that final confrontation with Nathan that left him bleeding out on the floor.

Nathan. I still couldn't believe it had been him. It had been more than a decade since I'd seen him, since I had even thought of him. For him to have been carrying all that crazy hatred inside for all that time boggled my mind, and he had unleashed the full brunt of it on the man sleeping next to me. The man I loved. My Steven.

I did love him, more than anything. The sexcapades of the previous week, from the stupid, coked-up threesome with Jesse and Colton, to the White Night encounter with Aaron, to that drunken four-way, and then that one last time with Aaron, none of it meant anything. Aaron didn't mean anything. Him showing up, back in my life, during all that had happened, had just messed with my already vulnerable emotions. We had spent six years together, six years, and I guess, one night.

That was all behind me now. Behind us. All the drugs, all the sex, it was done. My ring was on Steven's finger. Even if Nathan had been the one who put it there, Steven wore it, and I meant what it meant. We were for good, me and Steven. We had already endured the "for worse"; it was all "for better" from here on out.

He stirred in his sleep, and then sat up, bolted up more like, startled and panicked and gasping for air. I reached out to him, and he saw me, and I saw the fear fade from his face. It would take a while,

I knew, for him to believe he was safe again. Hearing him tell the police yesterday about everything Nathan had done to him, the abuse, the torture, it had broken my heart. He had had to endure that because of me. It was out of my past Nathan had come crawling, getting a sadistic revenge for an accidental adolescent touch (and for some not-so-accidental touches from his dad and dad's friends, it turned out). But still, it was my fault. Steven had had to suffer because of me, and I had my life to spend making it up to him.

I put my hand on his shoulder and he fell onto my chest, and we sat there, in his bed, and I held him tightly. I wouldn't let him go ever again.

"I love you," I said. "You're safe."

"I love you," he said. "I know." He was breathing easier now. "I forgot where I was for a moment. I thought . . ."

"I know what you thought. It's okay. It's going to take time."

"Thank you," he said. "I know I said it lots last night, but thank you. For finding me."

That was so Steven, to focus on me finding him rather than everything that had happened while he was gone. Everything had come out last night, the drugs and the sex and how Aaron had been masquerading as the Queen of Hearts at Wonderland. We were still numb and in shock, and it had just come out, added to the pile of stuff for us to deal with, later, when we were home, when we were safe, when Nathan was in jail.

I was so glad he wasn't dead. I hated him for what he had done, but I was glad I hadn't killed him. When the gun went off, I thought he was dead, and the thought that I had taken a life was almost too much.

"Are you hungry?" I asked. "Can I make you something to eat?"

"You don't cook," Steven said, with a smile on his face. "I'll cook."

"We could go out," I said. "It's Sunday morning. We could catch brunch at the Duchess."

"Not today," Steven said. "I . . . I can't . . . yet. Next week. Everyone will just have so many questions. I can't face that today."

"Okay. Whatever you want. We'll stay in."

"We'll have to talk to the police more," he said. "That will be bad enough, having to relive it all."

"We'll take it easy. You don't have to do anything until you're ready. No one expects you to."

"Thank you, Alex," he said again, and he wove his hand with mine. I could feel the ring on his finger.

Things would be okay.

Chapter 2

Saturday morning brunch at the Duchess was a tradition, and the boys were already there when we arrived. Jesse and Colton had brought along the boy they'd taken home from Wonderland the night before. He was a pretty little ginger kid, with a beard that seemed out of place on his baby face. They'd also brought along Walter, which I still had a problem with, but I was willing to overlook what he had done; God knows I had done enough things that were getting overlooked. Brandon was flying solo, having sworn off men in the week since he'd last seen Allan. Dinah and Christopher showed up just as we were sitting down, and there were hugs all around.

"I'd like to propose a toast," Jesse said, and we all lifted our mimosas. "Congratulations are definitely in order."

We clinked glasses around the table.

"Hey, did I miss a toast?" Aaron said, joining us.

"Sorry, darling," Jesse said, "but we couldn't wait."

"Well, let me catch up." He grabbed a mimosa from a passing waiter and raised his glass. "I just wanted to thank you for inviting me. I know this isn't easy but—"

"Hey! None of that! This is a happy occasion," Colton said. "You're not the Queen of Hearts here, so sit down and shush." He stuck out his tongue, and we laughed.

As we sat down, Steven squeezed my hand under the table, and I felt the ring there again. It had been his idea to invite Aaron to brunch, his idea to even go to brunch this week. He had to get things back to normal, he had said, and normal meant weekend brunches at the Duchess. It was where we went, all of us: Jesse and Colton, the Wonder Twins of Wonderland; Brandon, our favorite bartender and resident drama queen; my high school bestie Dinah and her fiancé Christopher . . . and Steven had insisted we include Aaron.

For his part in helping, Steven had said.

Sitting at the table, with Steven on my left and Aaron a few chairs over, was strange for me. When Aaron and I split up two years before, I never expected to see him again. I sure never expected to sleep with him again, and never would have guessed our connection would still be as strong as it was. I think Steven understood that. I hoped he knew it had nothing to do with what I felt for him.

We didn't talk about Aaron. We didn't talk about the White Night sex, high on E, or how the G that Allan had fed me had led me to a regrettable foursome with Aaron and the twins, or the even more regrettable and even more inexcusable night Aaron and I had spent together when I learned he was the Queen of Hearts, there on the fringe of my life for months.

There were lots of things we didn't talk about. It was probably for the best. Steven had to move past this. He was the one who had been kidnapped and tortured. He was the one who had to forget and heal. Did I want him to tell me every day that he forgave me for all I had done? Yes. Would I beg for him to do that? No.

My ring was on his finger. And that was all I needed to see.

Chapter 3

"Let's go to Wonderland tonight," Steven said.

"Really? Are you sure?"

"I'm sure. I miss having a life. We can't let what happened while I was gone change us completely. It's Saturday. Let's go drink and dance."

Wonderland, where the Hatter played his beats, where Brandon served his booze, where the Caterpillar sold his blow. Wonderland, where Jesse and Colton danced, two gods among many gods. Wonderland, where Aaron had performed all summer as the Queen of Hearts. Wonderland, where temptation lurked in every corner, along with a bit of regret and a whole lot of guilt.

"If you want to, sure, of course." What else could I say? He was probably thinking everything I was thinking. But he was the one who had suffered while I frolicked, and even if those frolics had been at Nathan's command, there was no excuse. Gin wasn't the reason. Cocaine wasn't the reason. Even Nathan wasn't the reason. I had fucked up.

"Text the guys," Steven said. "I'm going to go get pretty."

"You're always pretty." It was true. He was beautiful.

He smiled. "Love you."

I texted Jesse, Colton, and Brandon while Steven showered and changed. Their reaction was a collective "really? Already?" What could I say? Steven wanted to. Didn't they know I had to do whatever Steven wanted? Was I just convincing myself of that, though? The tightness in my chest wasn't about being at a club. It was about seeing the Caterpillar. He would be there, with his Baggies, and Steven would see him, and Steven would look at me, and his look would be disapproving.

And part of me wanted to taste that white-fire rush.

But no. Sampling the Caterpillar's wares had been fine when I was single, but it had nearly brought Steven and me to an end. No more. Never again.

Steven held my hand as we walked down the stairs into Wonderland. *Thump thump thump* went the bass and I tensed up. He looked at me and smiled. "It's good," he said. "We're good." He kissed my cheek and we were swallowed up by the crowds. Jesse picked me up and swung me around, and Colton did the same to Steven.

"So glad you guys are finally out and about again! We've missed you! Let's dance!"

They dragged us onto the dance floor, a tightly packed throng of eager disciples, swaying back and forth to the Hatter's music. He was there, in his booth, in his hat, and my eye met his, and he smiled. This hat was tall and green and white. Every night, a different hat.

We danced, and then had a drink, and then danced, and then had a drink, and a shot, and then danced, and drank, and danced and drank. It was like it was the first time, and there was no tension, and no drama, and no temptation. Just Steven and me, our friends, the music, and laughter. Why had I even been worried?

"Another drink?" Steven yelled to me over the music.

"Please," I said, "I'm just going to use the men's room."

"I'm glad we're here."

"Me too!"

He pulled me close and kissed me. My face flushed, and I was grinning like a fool as I went to the bathroom.

After I was done, I turned around at the urinal, and there he was: the Caterpillar.

"Hey," he said. "Long time, no see."

I ignored him and washed my hands.

"Oh, you're done again?" He had heard it before, and the tone in his voice was knowing.

"I don't want to talk to you."

"C'mon, Alex. What's one little bump?" He pulled a Baggie out of one of his many pockets and waved it in front of me. I saw a vision in my head, me reaching out, taking the bag, taking a bump, flying high as the white fire burned through me, Steven finding the bag, Steven screaming, Steven leaving me. Once I went down that rabbit hole, there was no coming back.

"Go away."

I walked out of the bathroom, vibrating. It was stupid, I told myself. It was fun, before. The fun was over. Craving it was ridiculous. I wasn't an addict.

I fought my way through the crowd, waving at Brandon behind the bar. Where had Steven got to? And why did his not being right there, right away, still send a panic through me? He wouldn't get kidnapped again. Nathan was in jail. He had pled guilty. There was no trial coming. It was over.

And there Steven was, talking to . . . Aaron?

Yes, we had hung out, all of us, brunches, a dinner party at Dinah's . . . but seeing Steven, talking to Aaron, Aaron's hand on Steven's shoulder, Steven's head thrown back in laughter as Aaron said something funny . . . Was I really jealous? Of course I was. There were only three men I had loved in my whole life, and this was two of them, and seeing them together, I thought of the third, and seeing Taylor's face in my mind reminded me of Nathan, and where, oh where, was the Caterpillar?

"Alex! There you are!" Steven grabbed my hand and pulled me over. "Look who I found! Here's your drink." He passed me my gin cran and I smiled and pushed down the fear and the jealousy. For Steven. I could be strong for Steven.

Chapter 4

Steven was gone when I woke up, and for a second, I panicked. Maybe I was coming out of another nightmare. In the month since Steven had come back, his sleep had gone back to normal. Mine, on the other hand, had taken a turn for the worse.

It was Nathan bringing up Taylor that had done it. I hadn't thought about Taylor in so long. I didn't let myself think about Taylor. He had been my first love, and he would always have a special place in my heart, and our time together had been cut short by him putting a gun to his head.

Nathan knew all about Taylor, and how much of a wreck I had been after Taylor died. Nathan showing up like he did, talking about Taylor like he had, it was as if the years since then had simply melted away. The pain was fresh, the pain of knowing Taylor was gone and the fear that I would always be alone.

But I wasn't alone. Steven was out for his morning run, like he did every day, and I was being stupid. I got out of bed and grabbed myself some water, and before I had even finished drinking it, Steven came in the door, panting and sweaty. He kissed me on the cheek.

"Morning, handsome," he said. "How did you sleep?"

"Great. You?" He didn't need to know. This, I could go through on my own. Steven had enough to deal with.

"Fancy some breakfast?"

"What are you making?"

"I was thinking French toast?"

"Sounds good. Can I help?"

Steven laughed. "You're kind of useless in the kitchen, handsome."

"Hey!" I said, feigning offense. I punched his arm playfully, and immediately wished I hadn't.

It was only for a second, and if I hadn't been looking right at him, I would have missed it, but I saw it, the instant I connected with him. It passed over his face, just a flinch of a shadow. But it was enough. I was an idiot! It had only been a month! Of course he would still be jumpy!

"I'm going to shower," Steven said. "I stink. I'll cook when I get out."

"Okay." Idiot, Alex! Idiot!

I stomped around the house, berating myself while Steven showered, and then sat there and made painfully meaningless chatter while he whipped up a yummy little breakfast for us. As he carried the plates over, I saw it. Or didn't see it, as the case was. His finger was bare.

"Where's your ring?" I asked, and regretted asking as soon as the words left my mouth.

"Oh, I took it off to shower," he said. "Guess I just forgot to put it back on."

It was a perfectly logical explanation, and there was no reason for me to disbelieve him.

We finished eating, and he got dressed for work as I cleaned up. He kissed me on the cheek as he went out the door and then I went to shower. The ring was still on the dresser.

He just forgot, I told myself. He would get to work and notice it wasn't there, and he would feel naked without it all day, and he would race home to put it on, and everything would be okay again. After everything we had gone through, everything would be okay again.

A week later, the ring still sat there on his dresser. I wouldn't bring it up again. He would put it on when he was ready. He had forgiven me so much. Surely I could be patient with him.

Chapter 5

It had been a long and hellish Friday at work. My boss at the bank had been very patient with everything we had gone through, and I was glad for that, but most of the time, he was a douche bag. Today, he had just kept piling on more and more work, when all I wanted to do was get home to Steven.

It had been two months, and the ring was still not back on. Tonight, I was going to ask him about it. I had almost asked, a few times. If he still loved me. He said he did, but didn't taking that ring off mean he didn't? That he didn't see us spending our lives together? And if we didn't end up together, after everything we had gone through, didn't that mean that Nathan had been right? That two men weren't meant to be married, weren't meant to be happy?

With all that going through my mind, more work on a Friday was the last thing I had wanted. I was cranky when I left work, and when I got to Steven's, I wasn't much better.

"Long day?" Steven said, as soon as he saw me. He knew me so well.

"Very."

"Wanna eat out? I don't feel like cooking."

"Whatever," I said, more snappishly than I had meant. "As long as there's gin." Steven looked hurt, and I immediately regretted my tone. "Sorry. Yes, let's go out. We've both had long weeks."

You're not a good person, Alex, I thought, as we got ready to go out. *Steven is the one who went through yada yada yada. How long are you going to beat yourself up for what Nathan did? Even if it was to* get *to you, it wasn't* you *who did it. You didn't beat him. You didn't hold him prisoner. All you did was go out and get drunk and get high and get fucked. Even if you did eventually get him back, you did a lot in that week.*

Dinner was quiet. I couldn't shake the dark and angry thoughts spiraling around my head, and seeing Steven's ringless finger just made me angry. Not at him. Never at him. And not at Nathan, like I should have been. Just at myself. If I hadn't fucked up so much, if I wasn't such a complete fuckup in every way one person could be a fuckup, Steven would be wearing my ring, we would be planning our wedding and our future. Everything would be good.

"What are you thinking?" Steven asked.

It was my opportunity. "Just about work," I lied, and the opportunity passed. He didn't need my shit on top of everything he must still be feeling. The ring, like Nathan, like Aaron, like cocaine, were topics best left avoided.

But as we left the restaurant that night, he took my hand, and right then, I didn't notice the missing ring. I rested my head on his shoulder as we walked home, and the doubt melted away. I loved him. He loved me. Things would be good again.

"Faggots!"

It was a shout from a car that sped off, and it jolted me from my dreams of happy-ever-after. That word. I *hated* that word.

"Alex," Steven said. "It's just a word. Don't worry about it. They're assholes. It's just a word." He knew how I felt about it. He knew what it triggered in me.

It wasn't just a word. It was everything wrong with the world, and everything wrong with us, and everything wrong with me. Steven didn't understand that, but the guys in that car knew. Nathan knew. I knew.

Chapter 6

I got home from work and Steven had dinner ready. There were candles on the table, a bottle of wine breathing. I took a breath too, thinking this was finally the end of what had gone before and the beginning of all that was to come. A big romantic dinner meant he would put the ring back on. We would resume our course toward big gay matrimony.

He kissed me on the cheek, and before I could stop myself, I asked, "What's the special occasion?"

"I just thought it was time we had a talk."

There was nothing then, is nothing now, and never will be anything good about *a talk.*

I pulled out a chair and slumped down into it, and my wedding plans derailed in my head. This was not a beginning.

He scooped out some salad and we ate in a sudden awkward silence.

"Look, I . . ." I said finally just as he said, "So here it is."

"Here what is?"

"I can't shake it. I have tried to shake it, but I can't."

"Shake what?"

"You and Aaron, and everything that happened, while I was gone."

While I was gone. What a cute euphemism to describe his week-long captivity and torture. And me and Aaron? That's what he couldn't shake? I sighed and said, "I told you, it didn't mean anything."

"It did, though."

"Okay it did, but it didn't mean as much as you think it did. It was an ending."

"An ending to something that had already ended."

"Yes." I was guilty, and guilt made me defensive, and defensiveness made me add, "And if you can't believe me, there's nothing else I can do to convince you."

"I do believe you."

"What then?"

He broke eye contact, and we ate some salad. Then he took a big gulp of his wine. "I think we should invite him over."

"What? Why?"

"Because I think I need to see it for myself."

"You've seen us together lots since then."

"No. I haven't seen you together." The emphasis he put on that last word made it clear what he meant.

"You want to watch me have sex with my ex?"

"No. I wasn't planning on just watching."

Of all the things Steven could have said, this was not one I ever would have predicted. Open relationships and frequent three-ways, that was Jesse and Colton. Steven hadn't ever even hinted he was interested in anything like that. "You want a threesome?"

"Maybe. I think. Yes."

"But why? Don't you think it would be awkward?"

"Maybe." He rubbed the back of my hand with his finger. "Don't you think it would be hot though too?"

I pictured the two of them together. I pictured the three of us together. It was hot, for sure. They both knew what I liked in bed, I knew what both of them liked. How could it be anything but hot? I could see myself in the middle, Steven on one side, Aaron on the other. My dick was suddenly hard in my pants.

"When were you thinking?"

"I was thinking, after dinner, maybe . . ."

"Excited?"

"Aren't you?" I took his hand, and guided it to my crotch. "Oh, you are." He smiled at me.

"I'll call after dinner."

Chapter 7

He kissed me, hard and long and passionately. He had always been an amazing kisser, right from our first kiss after our first date, that night so long ago when I backed into his car just to meet him. Since he was gone though, his kisses had a new intensity about them. Mine too, I suppose. It was a combination of relief and desperation and gratitude, and tonight, nerves and excitement.

There was a knock at the door.

"Do you want to let him in?" Steven asked.

"It's your house," I said, "and your idea."

"We'll just do it like we discussed. Play it by ear, have some wine, see where the night takes us. You're good with that?"

"Yes." And I was. Well, I was pretty sure I was. The man I loved. The men I loved? Me and two hot guys. The thought made my dick twitch again.

Steven opened the door. "Hey, come on in."

Aaron entered and I took them both in. I had a type, that was for sure. They were both the wholesome, All-American, boy-next-door gay-clone type, Aaron's hair a bit darker, Steven a bit more muscled. In my mind's eye, I undressed them, seeing Steven's closely trimmed chest hair, Aaron's smooth torso, following identical treasure trails to their two equally beautiful cocks.

There were hugs all around, and Steven brought us all a glass of wine and turned on the stereo. We small-talked, about each other's weeks, the latest gossip from Wonderland. An hour passed, and the bottle was empty. Steven went to uncork another.

"So what prompted this?" Aaron asked. "We never hang out at home on a Friday."

"We just weren't in the mood for Wonderland."

"The boys didn't want to come?"

"We didn't ask them," Steven said, coming back into the living room with the bottle and filling up all our glasses before sitting back down on the couch next to me.

"Well, cheers," Aaron said, and lifted his glass. We clinked, sipped. "I'll be right back," he continued. "Just need to pee."

Aaron disappeared down the hall.

"Do you think he's even into it?" I asked.

"How could he not be?" Steven said, his hand suddenly kneading my crotch.

"So do we just ask him?"

"Eager, are we?"

"Well, if we're going to do it, we might as well do it before we get too drunk."

Steven smiled and leaned in to kiss me, his hand never leaving my now hard dick. Our tongues danced in each other's mouths.

"Bad time?"

We pulled apart as Aaron came back into the room. He was standing there, a half grin on his face.

"No, actually," Steven said. "Perfect timing." He patted the couch next to him. "Come sit."

Aaron raised an eyebrow, and my breathing quickened. He grabbed his wine from the table near the chair he'd been in before, and sat down next to Steven on the couch. "What's up, guys?"

"We've been thinking," Steven said.

"What about?"

"I'll let Alex tell you. I'll be right back. Need to use the boys' room myself."

He went down the hall, leaving me alone with Aaron. My ex. My ex of six years. My ex I'd had those extra-complicated and semi-recent hookups with. My ex I was about to have a three-way with.

"What's up, Alex?" he asked.

I swallowed hard, and slid over next to him, and kissed him. He kissed back, briefly, then pushed me back. "What's going on?"

"Want to have some fun?"

"Are you serious?"

"Yah, we are."

"Do you think it's smart?"

"I don't know. Let's find out." I kissed him again, and his hesitation crumbled, and he kissed me back harder, and I let out a small moan as his hand pulled me tight against his face.

I got so caught up in kissing Aaron that I barely noticed Steven come back into the room until I felt the couch shift. I broke apart the kiss and looked at him looking at Aaron. Their eye contact barely wavered as he pulled my face to his and kissed me. Could he taste Aaron on my lips?

Aaron's mouth was on my neck to my right. Steven started kissing down my neck to the left. I had one arm around each of their shoulders, barely believing this was happening. I was no stranger to threesomes, but this, this was Aaron and Steven. Together! I looked down to see their lips meeting, right in front of my face. And then the three of us were kissing, all together, and it was a melting mess of mouths.

Steven stood up and took his shirt off. Aaron murmured appreciatively at Steven's chest, and we all chuckled. Then Steven reached over me to undo the buttons on Aaron's shirt, and as I watched my current lover slowly undress my ex-lover, I started to undo Steven's pants. He leaned across me and his mouth covered Aaron's nipple. Aaron's head rolled back with a groan; he had always loved nipple play. Steven looked up at him, then looked back at me. His dick was hard in his pants, and I pulled it free. He groaned.

"Maybe we should move this to the bedroom," he said, and he stood up, pulling us both to our feet. He kissed me, then Aaron, then me again, and as we clumsily stumbled toward the bedroom, we finished undressing each other.

In the bedroom, Steven pushed me onto the bed. I looked back at him, at them, standing there, both nude, both hard-bodied and hard-cocked. Then Steven pushed Aaron down to the bed as well, and I attacked his mouth. Steven climbed down next to me, and they were each working one of my nipples. Their hands traced my thighs, and then both of them had their hands on my balls and cock. First Steven's mouth, then Aaron's mouth, then both their mouths. I bucked my hips. I had never been so turned on.

I held their heads there at my dick, on my dick. My fingers tangled in their hair. One would work my shaft, the other my balls, then they'd switch. It was heaven.

I looked down to see them kissing again, and took the moment to catch my breath. I didn't want this to end so soon, and the two of them, both knowing all the spots and techniques to drive me crazy, already had me on the edge.

They looked up at me, and Aaron slid up to press his lips to mine, as Steven started sucking me again. First me, then Aaron. I felt a twinge of something, seeing my ex's dick in my lover's mouth, but Aaron's mouth on mine drove the thought away. I felt Steven slither up to the top of the bed, his dick pulsing against me.

We were three-in-one, hands and mouths and cocks. Our bodies were slick with sweat and our groans and moans filled the air. I went down on Aaron and looked up to see him and Steven kissing, slow, savory kisses. A surge of jealousy ran through me, seeing them, but I closed my eyes and inhaled Aaron's dick. He thrust his hips into my mouth and I felt him tense, felt Steven tense next to me feeling Aaron tense.

"I want to fuck you."

I had heard that from Aaron so many times, and the thought of him fucking me, of Steven seeing him fuck me, had my dick pre-cumming, had me clambering up and onto my stomach. And then I looked over, and Aaron's hands were playing with Steven's ass. Steven arched his back, and Aaron rolled onto his knees, lapping at Steven's ass.

"Fuck me," Steven told him, and Aaron slid his cock up and down Steven's crack. Steven *never* wanted to bottom, and being more of a bottom myself, I didn't mind, but this? He was practically begging for it.

I suddenly felt so exposed, so ignored. Aaron reached over to the nightstand, grabbed the lube and a condom. He leaned down over Steven's body, tight together, as he ripped the condom open. I lay there watching, my dick suddenly limp. Aaron slid into Steven, and I watched Steven's face, the absolutely ecstasy on it, mouth half open, eyes half closed. Slowly, slowly, Aaron went deeper, deeper, until he was leaning down on Steven's back, and they kissed again.

"I guess I'm not needed here anymore." As soon as I said the words, I regretted it.

They both looked at me. "Well, come over here," Steven said.

"No, you guys are good." I stood up and grabbed a blanket to wrap around my nakedness.

Aaron pulled out and I heard Steven gasp as the dick left his ass. "I told you this wouldn't work. I knew he couldn't handle it, Steven."

"What?" My jaw dropped. "This was planned?"

"Well, yes, we talked about it before I talked to you about it."

"What the fuck, Steven? Why?"

"I thought you wanted it, Alex."

"Fuck you. You're clearly the one who wants this."

"Alex, calm down."

They were both standing there naked, still hard. They had planned this? Between them? Who knew what else they had talked about? Who knew what else they had done? Had they done this before? Was that why they fit together so naturally?

"No, I won't calm down! When did you guys plan this? Have you fucked before?"

"Jesus, Alex, you're out of line. This was for you!"

"Don't fucking lie to me, Steven! You're the one who just had his dick in your ass. This was for you!"

Bam! I had barely seen him move, but I surely felt his slap. My face was on fire, my head ringing.

"How fucking dare you! After everything you did while I was gone? You're accusing me of cheating? Are you fucking nuts?"

"Go to hell, Steven."

I stormed out of the bedroom, slamming the door. They didn't come after me. "Let him go," I heard Aaron say. I got dressed. They didn't come after me. "Good-bye, assholes!" I yelled out, and left. I couldn't believe it! How had that happened so quickly? How did it go from glory to this, this fist that had reached through my chest and squashed my heart? My eyes were on fire from tears I wouldn't let fall.

I started walking home, suddenly feeling a lot more drunk than I had. How many bottles of wine had we had? Three? Four?

No. This wasn't going to end this easily.

I turned around and went back. I froze with my hand on the doorknob. I walked around the side of Steven's house, to his bedroom window. I looked inside. They were there, on the bed, still naked, Steven wrapped in Aaron's arms.

I was a fool. It was done, and there was nothing there for me.

"Fine," I said aloud, as I walked off again. "They can have each other. There's a bar filled with men, and my ass is theirs for the asking."

Chapter 8

"Alex, my friend, so nice to hear from you!"

I was too hung over for the Caterpillar's niceties. "Can you swing by?"

"Already?"

"Rough night. Rough week."

"Be there in twenty, my friend."

I hung up and stared at my laptop screen, open to Facebook. Remove Steven Thompson as a friend? Had it come to this? In just a few weeks? Had it already been a few weeks? Had it *only* been a few weeks, since that disastrous attempt at a three-way? Time was either moving too fast, or too slow, and nothing was making sense anymore. Curiouser and curiouser and furiouser and furiouser.

It was all such a blur, the threesome, its aftermath at Wonderland, and the long and lonely nights since. Every night, I had come home to an apartment empty except for Griffin. Griffin and gin. Only drunk did the image of them together go away. Only drunk did I forget the scene I had caused at the club after.

I hadn't talked to anyone. Jesse and Colton had tried to get in touch, but I'd been ignoring them. The way I had treated them was unforgivable. If Facebook was the last connection to the outside world, removing Steven, the last of my group of actual friends, was the last step. Then it would just be me and my cat and my gin.

Griffin meowed at me and I picked him up and held him close. There was no need to cry. It was better this way. I wouldn't get hurt, and I sure wouldn't be able to hurt anyone else. All I had to do was go on about my life. Go to work. Come home. Get drunk. Go to bed. Go to work. Repeat. Fun outside the apartment was done.

My intercom went off, and I buzzed him up, my new best friend. My only friend. My dealer. The Caterpillar.

"Alex, you're looking good."

"Thanks," I said, taking money out of my pocket and slapping it down on the counter.

"All business tonight, my friend," he said, as he counted the cash. "So much? Someone is having a party."

"Just me," I said. Maybe it was a lot at a time. I didn't want to run out. This would make me happy. This would make me forget.

He handed the Baggies to me, one by one. "Always a pleasure," he said. "We'll see you again."

I wanted to strangle him, anything to wipe that smugness off his face. He had known I would be back. He was right. I was wrong. I was always wrong. Wrong about this. Wrong about Steven. Wrong about life.

I didn't strangle him though, just said good-bye and locked the door behind him. I poured out the first Baggie onto a mirror, cut it up into lines, and started my weekend.

Later.

My heart was racing as I swiped through Grindr profiles. There had to be someone out there, someone just looking for an ass to pound. I was that ass. I didn't even care if he was particularly hot. I wouldn't see his face. He could just shove me into the pillows and plow me from behind. I didn't care. I just had to be fucked.

Swipe. Swipe. Snort. Swipe. Swipe.

Later.

He was gone, and good. I suddenly couldn't stop crying.

I could still feel him in my ass though, HngTop34. Not as hung as I would have hoped, but it had done the job.

Should I find another? It was early. I had booze. I had drugs. I had nothing left to lose. I swiped through the profiles. I had seen all these before. There was no one new. And no one like Steven anyway.

Steven. Maybe I should call him. Would he be awake still? Just coming home from Wonderland? Had he been dancing? With Aaron maybe? Maybe they were fucking. They were probably fucking. Right now.

I dialed his number. "Fuck you, Steven. I can get fucked too. You should've seen him. He was black and built and he fucked me hard. Fuck you."

I shouldn't have left that message. Fuck. Why did I do such stupid things? Swipe. Swipe. Snort. Swipe.

Still later.

I just wanted to sleep. My dick was sore. My nose hurt. My heart was pounding too fast. Like the guy had pounded me too fast.

Had I really just had another random guy come over? Two in one night? I wondered if Masc4Masc could tell that HngTop34 had been there before him. I wondered if he cared. More gin. That would help me sleep.

But first, Aaron.

"Hope you like my seconds, you asshole. What a fucking waste. You both fucking suck."

I needed to not have my phone turned on. That was the problem. If I turned it off, I wouldn't keep leaving these messages. It was four in the morning. I just wanted to sleep.

At least I wasn't thinking about Steven anymore.

Oh. Wait.

Chapter 9

It had been a long and hellish Friday at work, and I wanted nothing more than to get home and pour myself a very generous gin and cran, but no, that was not to be. My dear and darling fag hag Dinah was getting married in a week, and tonight was her bachelorette party. And of course, good little fagcessory that she was, she was having it at Wonderland. Wonderland was the last place I wanted to be tonight. I would have been perfectly happy staying in and getting comfortably numb, but I was Best Bridesman and had to be there.

I loosened my tie on the elevator up to my condo, stretching the kinks out of my neck. Why did this party have to be tonight? What were the chances I could get her drunk enough quickly enough that I could leave her with her other friends and sneak back home? Doubtful. "Stupid fucking wedding!" I said to myself, not for the first time that day.

The elevator doors opened and there was my neighbor from across the way, Walter, who had lost a lot of weight recently thanks to our friend Jesse's personal training program. He still sported the ridiculous mustache that had caused me to nickname him Walrus, though.

"Hey, Alex," he said, "rough day?"

"Does it show?"

"You just don't seem your normal self lately."

Normal self. What was that again? It had been a long time since I'd felt normal, been a long time since life had been normal. The past six months had been . . . complicated. "Getting better every day though," I said, which was a lie but I wasn't in the mood for a long discussion.

He must've picked up on my short temper. Normally, he would chatter away until I missed the time he was nothing more than the cranky asshole who used to sneer and swear at me. Now, he just said a quick good-bye and got into the elevator.

Griffin bounded out at me as soon as I opened the door, a big cuddly ball of brown and black. Not even he was enough to put a smile on my face, though. Was there really no way to get out of this bachelorette party? Dinah herself hated when straight girls brought their parties to the gay bar. We were her gays, Dinah always said, and she didn't want to share us with every roly-poly straight girl come looking for a GBF.

Wonderland. In the past year, that club had given me some of the happiest, horniest, most horrifying memories of my life. And I had to go. She was my bestie since high school, and this was important to her. She had stood by me through coming out, through a relationship, through a breakup, and through all of the shit that had happened this past year when Steven was kidnapped. Through all of it, she had stood by me.

I had to be there for her now.

But first things first, if I was going to face Wonderland again, there was no way I could do it sober. I scrolled through my phone until I found the Caterpillar's number and called him. "Sup," he said. "Want a visit?"

"If you don't mind."

"For you? Don't mind at all. Be there in twenty."

I waited for him to arrive, and was on my second stiff double when the buzzer rang. Soon, he was up, and it was my money for his coke. "Thanks, Alex," he said. "I didn't expect to be back here this quick."

"Don't judge me," I said, angrily, but then, it had only been two days since his most recent visit. Maybe I should be judged. But not by him.

"Oh, I'm not judging. You, my friend, have become one of my favorite customers," and he was off again, into the night, to visit whoever was next on his list of fiending fans needing a fix.

I pulled the mirror out of the coffee table drawer, and poured out a pile of the pure white powder. I crushed it flatter, separated it into two fat lines with the razor blade that was already all waiting for me. It was that common now, I just kept the paraphernalia I needed right there. The chances of anyone coming over and seeing it were pretty slim, after all. I had made sure of that.

The first sniff of the weekend was wonderful. It was white fire filling my brain and my heart seemed to pause, and then I gasped. I finished off the first line, and looked down at my reflection in the mirror. This was my life now. This is what I did. Even if I hadn't been going to Wonderland, I still would have called the Caterpillar over. When the gin was nearly drunk, and I was clearly drunk, and when some guy off Grindr was on his way over, I would have called the Caterpillar to set up a little party and play, because that's what happens when you take everything that is wonderful in your life and wreck it with a series of progressively stupid choices.

You forget however you have to forget.

Tonight, there would be no Grindr boys. There would just be real boys. They would all be there at Wonderland, because it was Friday and that's where they went. Brandon would be working behind the bar. Jesse and Colton would be dancing. Steven . . . oh yes, Steven would probably be there too. What would he say if he knew how bad things had gotten since we called it off? If he knew I drank myself to sleep every night without him, and coked myself into oblivion and orgasm every weekend?

How could he hate me more than he already did?

Would he be there tonight? Dinah hadn't said, and I hadn't asked. Aaron would be there though, and if Aaron was there, Steven probably wouldn't be far away. They could say there was nothing between them, but I knew what I had seen, and it had been weeks now. Who knows? Maybe they were official now. The two men I had loved the most, loving each other.

I inhaled the second line and vibrated. I was flying now. Only that high could I be safe. Only that high could I face them, could I face Wonderland.

Chapter 10

It hadn't always filled me with dread, that magical club called Wonderland.

When Steven had first taken me there, on our first night together, so long ago now, I had been enchanted by its whimsy and its magic and its men. Even though I was so into Steven, there were gorgeous men all around me. And the men and the music and the merriment made it easily the most incredible gay bar I had ever set foot in. Way better than sad old Trix back home.

Wonderland had become a part of our relationship. It was where we went to unwind from our week, where we went to drink and dance with our friends. It was a home away from our homes, and we were stars there, and we were in love.

All that changed though, when Steven got kidnapped. Well, before, I guess. I looked back now, and I saw the coke use creeping up on me. It was not a new problem, now, but it was my new solution. Back then, it had been so very once in a while. But Steven hated drugs and when Steven found drugs on me, we had had what was then our worst fight ever. If only that had stayed our worst fight.

It was at Wonderland I had bought the drugs that caused that first breakup, and it was to Wonderland I went after that breakup, to lose myself again in gin and cocaine and, eventually, in a disastrously stupid threesome with Wonderland's Wonder Twins, Jesse and Colton. We'd all been friends, but they were a lot more sexually open, and that night, with nothing left to lose, I went along with it, gladly, willingly, hornily.

That could have been bad enough, but then Steven went missing, and in the week that followed, as I was stalked and harassed and tormented by calls from his kidnapper, that one night of indiscretion became something more. During that week, Aaron resurfaced, my long-ago and long-forgotten ex. And my confusion and my frustration and my inebriation led to a few encounters that should never have happened, that stirred up a whole bunch of feelings that should have stayed buried.

When I got Steven back, we were just so happy to have it over with that we tried to forget it all ever happened. Steven was the one who insisted we include Aaron in our lives. He joined our little circle, and there at Wonderland, how amazing it was that everything would be fine from that point forward, like all that meaningless fucking, like all that meaningful loving, had never happened, and that the kidnapping had never happened, and that the drugs had never happened, and like the proposal had never happened.

And then it happened, That Friday Night . . . one Friday night just like tonight, when I had to go back there, for the first time since that night. No. I couldn't let myself think about it. It would psych me out of going and I had to be there tonight. For Dinah.

I scraped up what was left on the mirror and snorted it back. Time to shower and change, and then maybe one more line, getting high before going down once more, to Wonderland.

Chapter 11

Dinah met me outside. Even though it was her night, she knew how nervous I was, knew I hadn't been back since That Friday Night. She looked radiant, even with her tacky plastic tiara. Maybe she had found the real love of her life in Twitten (okay, in Christopher) . . . maybe she would be the exception to the rule. Maybe she would get her happy-ever-after.

The little voice inside me that said that that was because she was straight, the little voice inside me that said that I would never have it because I wasn't straight, I told that little voice to fuck right off. It was with me a lot these days though, part Taylor's voice, part Nathan's. All I could hope was that the Friday night beats of the Hatter in Wonderland would drown out its insistent nagging.

"Thanks for coming," she said, wrapping her arms around me. Instinctively, I picked her up and spun her around, and for a second, I didn't want to let her go. We'd been through a lot, me and her.

"Wouldn't miss it for anything, love," I said.

"Come meet the girls," she said, taking me by my hand and leading me down the stairs.

The music was generic, fast and thumping hard, and my heartbeat sped up in response (to the music or the blow, I wasn't sure, but in response). Immediately, I looked around to see where they all were: Jesse and Colton, Brandon, Aaron, Steven . . . but I couldn't see any of them. The dance floor was packed tight, the lines at the bar were long, the Hatter was in his new booth, a balcony overlooking the floor.

Dinah introduced me to her gaggle of girlfriends. I'd heard about them all before, but was only now putting faces to the gossip. Sure, we talked about her straight friends from her straight life, but she kept me and the gayborhood for her, and I was fine with that. We had enough to deal with in our own world, without them coming down. Stacy with the Cuban lover. Amanda who had just landed herself a rich husband. Samantha, who'd recently given birth to a second perfect baby. The names went in one ear and out—I had my hag, and one was plenty, even if I did love her to death. Eventually, all gay boys and their hags separated—Dinah's wedding would lead to Dinah's pregnancy and that would be the end of our adventures in Wonderland.

Really, Alex? After all you two have been through? Do you really think that? Was it inevitable, that she would leave like everyone else had left? Of course it was. And then, I would be alone.

"Let me go get us shots," I said without thinking, and was halfway to the bar before I saw Brandon, all blond and abs and memories of his sketchy little ex, Allan. I did a quick about-face and headed to the side bar. It was safer. Tim, the side bar guy, in no way figured in to any of the mistakes of my semi-recent past. He was bookish, kinda plain-looking, boring as fuck, quite frankly.

Maybe Walter was right and I was shallow. Tim still served drinks just as well as anyone else. Did it matter that Brandon was ten times hotter, with the most cut abs I had ever seen on anyone, and an absolutely perfect valley of butt crack poking out from his Andrew Christians?

"Six tequilas," I told Tim, and he smiled and started to pour. I turned around as he did, checking out the club from an angle I didn't normally see it from. Yes, there they were, on their dance box on the packed dance floor, two perfect specimens of gayness. Wonderland's Wonder Twins: Jesse and Colton. What was with Colton's uber-douchey chinstrap, though? That was new, and shot to shit the looking-like-twins thing.

I paid for the tequila, which Tim had been nice enough to put on a tray for me, along with a handful of lime wedges. Fighting my way back to Dinah and the girls, I kept glancing about, dreading the moment when someone would see me, or when I'd see him. Either of him, actually, Aaron or Steven. There may be no X in Wonderland, but there was always an ex at Wonderland. It was the nature of the gayborhood, and I wasn't ready to face either of them yet.

"Shots!" one of the girls squealed and started handing them out as I put the tray down on the table. "Hey, there's too many," she said.

I grabbed the extra and tipped it back. Dinah shook her head. "Alex, are you okay?"

"Absolutely, bride-to-be," I lied. "Let's do these."

The tequila burned, and two back to back was almost too much for me. I had the coke baggie in my pocket, with a bit left over, and the Caterpillar would be along soon if I needed a little more powdered sobriety. The girls flocked to the dance floor as the Hatter mixed in some Britney. I stayed, both to guard the table and to avoid the twins. They'd tried to get ahold of me after That Friday Night, but I had ignored their calls. When the passive-aggressive status war ended between me and Steven on Facebook, I'd deactivated all my social media, and blocked them on Grindr. I hadn't talked to them since. I just wanted to get through the night without seeing them, without seeing Brandon, without seeing . . .

There he was. Steven. Did he count as an ex-fiancé, or just an ex? Sure, he had worn the engagement ring I'd bought for him, but it had been put there by Nathan, not me, while Nathan had us tied to chairs. Hardly a real, romantic proposal. Was Nathan right about gay marriage? Was it just not for us?

Steven looked good, he always had. My heart ached and my body tensed and my eyes brimmed with tears I refused to let fall. Maybe he wasn't the gorgeous perfection of the twins, and no one had Brandon's abs, but he had been mine. From the moment I saw him getting into his white VW Rabbit to our first night dancing at Wonderland, through a summer of exceedingly perfect moments . . . until Nathan kidnapped him and Aaron came back into my life, and everything got all fucked up.

Our eyes met across the room, the way they had once met across a parking lot, but this time, the smile that was on his face fell. Just for a second, but long enough for me to notice. He had to know I'd be there. Dinah had been my friend first, of course. But the smile came back as he came toward us, and she squealed and jumped into his arms, just as she had squealed and jumped into mine. He even swung her around the same way I had, as well as he could in a crowded bar.

And then he set her down and turned to me. "Hey, Alex," he said. It was almost with a sigh. A sad, disappointed sigh.

"Hey."

"How's things?"

Hell. Shit. Fucked up. How do you think things are, Steven? "Fine. And for you?"

"Things are good. You look good."

It was a lie. I knew it was a lie, and he knew I knew it was a lie. It was one of those lies we tell because we don't know what else to say. "Thanks," I replied. "You too." That wasn't a lie. He did look good. And it wasn't fair that he looked good, happy, handsome, when I was falling apart and a total wreck, inside and out. Maybe it was time for me to dip into my Caterpillar leftovers.

"Steven!"

"About time!"

The twins descended upon us, and there were more hugs and laughter, and then they turned to me.

"Hey, Alex," Colton said. "How—"

"Don't." Jesse cut Colton off. "He made his choice."

Jesse turned his back to me, and Colton, with a sad half smile, did the same. Steven looked at me and sadly shook his head, and then they were off to the bar for drinks. I blinked away the tears.

"You okay?" Dinah asked me, as her girls cheered the go-go boy who suddenly was on the dance box above us. I was all too aware of his crotch practically level with my face.

"I'm fine, I just need to go to the bathroom quick."

"You don't need to do that, Alex," she said. There was no point in denying. She knew exactly why I wanted to disappear.

"It'll make things easier." That was a lie too, one that she didn't believe, one that I didn't believe. But a necessary lie, because if it didn't help, then I was just a messy addict, and that was too real. Addiction. The word stuck in my head. "I'll be able to celebrate with you."

"I just want you here. I don't need you partying."

"Dinah. I have to."

Her look was as sad as Colton's or Steven's. Why couldn't they just be mad like Jesse? Mad was easier to handle than disappointed. I couldn't face that look.

I fought my way through the crowd to the bathroom, not even waiting until I was in a stall before I had the Baggie out, flicking it to loosen the powder inside. I dipped a key in and pulled out the last of it, luckily a bigger heap than I'd expected. One big sniff later, and this was a burn I liked. Not like tequila, not like tears. Just the white fire rush of cocaine.

Chapter 12

When I got back to Dinah's table, the girls were all dancing, and it was just me and Steven. We sat there, silent in the noise. I watched the crowd, watched the Hatter, watched anything but the guy across the table from me. The guy I had been planning on spending the rest of my life with. The guy who had suffered for me and been betrayed by me, and then made everything worse, That Friday Night.

"So, where's Aaron?" The words were out before I could stop them.

"Alex, let's not do this."

"Just making conversation."

"Alex, there is nothing between me and Aaron."

I was suddenly on my feet, my mind filled with the flashing images of That Friday Night. Hands. Mouths. Their naked bodies. "Steven, don't fucking lie to me. I know, Steven. I'm not a fucking retard. Of course there's something going on between you guys."

"Alex, sit down. Don't you dare make this about you! Can't you let Dinah have one night?"

"Oh yeah, I forgot, it's all about me being selfish, isn't it? Because my feelings don't matter."

"Oh fuck off, Alex. It's always all about your feelings." Steven slammed his beer onto the table and walked away.

I sat back down, grabbed his beer, and tipped it back. It was cold, and there, and the least he could do. That man I was supposed to spend the rest of my life with. That man I was supposed to love. That man who was supposed to love me. If he could have my ex, I could have his beer. Fair trade, no? Even Steven.

"What happened, Alex?" Dinah said, appearing from the crowd, shaking her head.

"What do you mean?"

"Steven's leaving. Did you . . ."

"Oh sure, it's of course my fault. Steven couldn't have done anything wrong. Maybe he's running home to fuck Aaron."

"Goddammit, Alex!" Dinah never got mad, not at me, but this was her mad face, and I didn't like it one bit. "There is nothing going on between Steven and Aaron. Stop making everything about yourself and for one fucking second, try to think of someone else. Stop being such a melodramatic fag!" Her face went white and she raised a hand to her lips to stop the words it was already too late to take back.

The club seemed to stop, and all I could see was her. "What did you call me?"

"I didn't mean it like that, I—"

"Fuck you, Dinah, fuck you."

I pushed past her and into the crowd. "Alex!" she called from behind me, but I ignored her. I ignored her posse of girlfriends flocking back to her from the dance floor. I ignored Jesse and Colton at the bar with Brandon, looking at me, judging me. I ignored the people dancing, I ignored the people laughing. I headed straight toward the Caterpillar, there now, on his stool. I exchanged my money for his drugs, and as the Hatter shot off Wonderland's new glitter cannon above the dance floor, I left it behind me, left them all behind me.

I had said it before, but this time I meant it. I was done with Wonderland.

Chapter 13

It was called the Hole, and that's all it was. A trashy, dark, and tiny little bar, blocks away from the glitter and glow of Wonderland. It was filthy, to be honest, and I'd normally never go there. But leaving Wonderland, I couldn't face the total loneliness of home, and as the warmth of the cocaine filled me, I wanted nothing more than more booze and some cock.

The Hole had a back room, and there, in the dark, I could bend over for some stranger and have him fuck me senseless. A faceless, nameless fuck, devoid of all meaning, rough and raw and totally self-destructive. Let Dinah have her fun. Let the boys have their dance floor of smooth, hard-bodied, beautiful men. Let Steven have Aaron. None of that mattered. Not to me. Not anymore.

In the darkness of the Hole, I ordered a double gin and sat in the shadows, watching the men watch me. It was a different kind of watching than at Wonderland. There, it was gods judging gods. Here, we were all fallen. The pretension was stripped away, and we bared ourselves. We were here in the squalor for one thing and one thing only.

I felt the eyes on me before I saw him, bearded and dark, leaning up against the wall, one hand on his beer, one hand on his bulge. He saw me seeing him, and raised his beer in salute. He wasn't my type. I didn't go for face fur, and he had to have a decade on me at least. But he was there, and I could tell he wanted me.

I walked past him into the bathroom, and felt his eyes follow me. In the stall, I fortified myself with a heaping helping of the Caterpillar's finest, and looked at myself in the mirror. I loathed what I saw.

He was standing outside the bathroom when I left, and I had to rub against him to get through the door. His hand grabbed my ass as I passed, his fingers digging in, looking for entry. I headed to the back, looking over my shoulder as I went into the dim, blue-lit room, where strangers screwed in shadows. He followed me in.

He pushed me up against the wall, his beard rough and ripping at my mouth. The contact was good, hard and savage enough to drive away anything and anyone from my mind. He pushed me to my knees, and I clawed frantically at his belt and zipper, pulling out his thick slab of meat, which was already hard and leaking. "Eat me," he said, and shoved his dick into my mouth. I gagged before finding my rhythm. His fingers tangled in my hair as he pushed himself into me. I could feel my eyes water as he fucked my face so hard I could barely breathe.

Suddenly, he pulled me to my feet, and spun me around. He yanked my pants to the ground and his fingers clawed into my ass. His spit on my hole was cold and wet from his beer, and he pushed my face against the brick wall as he pushed his dick inside me. I groaned as he penetrated me. No gentle entry, no slow and steady. He fucked me hard and fast and furious, faster and faster, furiouser and furiouser, his hands on my hips, and suddenly again, he pulled out and I felt him shoot on my back. "Thanks," he said, and he pulled up his pants and walked away.

I felt tears on my face, as hot and wet as his load. I could make out the people around me, some who had been watching, go back to their own acts. What did they think of me? Did it matter? Not to me. Not as long as I was flying high and safe on cocaine wings. Nothing could touch me. I pulled up my pants and went back into the main bar, semen dripping past the waistband. There was plenty of time before last call.

Chapter 14

I woke up in the loving arms of a massive hangover. The rest of the night was a blur. Through the throb in my head, vague images floated. Sucking off a leather daddy in the bathroom. Getting cut off and screaming at the bartender. Doing coke in the park on the stumble home. Puking in the middle of the street.

"Way to keep things classy, Alex," I told myself. I was wobbly on my feet as I went to the fridge and gulped down water straight from the jug I kept in there for just such emergencies. My stomach lurched, and the sun was bright through the window. The clock read four-thirty. Had I really slept the entire day? What time had I gotten home? It couldn't have been much past two. . . .

I looked at my phone, dreading the sent messages I'd find, but luckily, there weren't any (unless drunk Alex was now covering his tracks so sober Alex wasn't horrified) (no, if I'd been cut off at the Hole of all places, I hadn't been coherent enough to think of that). At least I hadn't drunk-texted Aaron or Steven. In the past few months, that had happened once or twice when the cycle of self-loathing and substance use had hit a special low.

There were, however, a series of texts from Dinah, apologizing for her *fag* slip-up. She knew how that word hit me. Even if she'd shortened it to *fag,* which maybe wasn't as bad (*maybe*), it was still *faggot.* It was still bullies on bicycles, and it was still beer bottles thrown from cars, and it was still Nathan, violent and hate-filled and holding us captive.

I could still see him lying there, after the gun went off. Thinking he was dead, hoping he was dead. He deserved to die. After all he'd done, all the pain he'd caused. My wonderful life had exploded, and he'd lit the fuse.

Later, I'd been glad he hadn't died. When it came out what had happened to him as a kid, that his dad had raped him, that his dad had let friends rape him, I couldn't help but feel sympathy. Somewhat. But when I thought of what Nathan had cost me, about how it destroyed me and Steven, about how it destroyed me and everyone, I wanted him to rot where he was.

That's where Dinah's *fag* had sent me . . . back to all those dark places. It was her fault I'd ended up at the Hole. Fuck her. Fuck her precious little Twitten and their precious little straight marriage. It was too early in my hangover for that kind of anger, unless I had a little something left over.

"What do you think?" I asked Griffin, as he came rubbing against my leg and meowing. "Does Daddy have any coke left?"

I found my jeans, went through the pockets, sighed that there was nothing. I checked my jacket pockets, but was equally disappointed. Did I need to call the Caterpillar? So early in the day? Maybe I could sleep off the hangover. Then I wouldn't need the little wake-me-up pick-me-up.

But it was too late. My thoughts had already gone dark, and when I closed my eyes, I lived it again. The fear when Steven went missing. The confusion of the days that followed. The terror and the violence of that final confrontation with Nathan. And then That Friday Night, the nakedness, the betrayal, the ecstasy and the agony and the jealousy, and then my emotional meltdown at Wonderland.

Being there last night brought it all back and fresh. I didn't remember getting there That Friday Night, the pain and the rage of seeing them together was so fresh. But I remembered pounding back shot after shot in seconds. I remembered Brandon's concern even as he served them to me. I remembered the Caterpillar, passing me a freebie. It gets a bit blurry then, the lines off the table, security asking me to leave, me going all Real Housewife Teresa and flipping the table, punching Brandon as he tried to calm me down. And then I was on the pavement outside just as Jesse and Colton arrived, and when they tried to help, the last of the bile exploded from me.

"It's all your fault!" I screamed. "You made everything so sexual, you changed everything! And now . . . and now . . ." I couldn't tell them what had happened.

"Alex, chill the fuck out," Jesse said.

"We didn't make you do anything you didn't want to do."

Colton's words echoed Nathan's too closely and I threw myself at him, swinging. Jesse pulled me off and tossed me to the ground.

"You're fucking whores! You're both total fucking sluts! I hate you! I hate you both! I wish I'd never met you!"

That part stood out clear, and then everything went black until I woke up, broken, ashamed, and weighed down with the guilt of it all. I rejected their attempts to reach out. They were gone from my life, all of them. I was done with it all.

It was just me and Griffin and, maybe once in a while, Dinah.

Oh, and one more person.

"Hey, it's me," I told the Caterpillar, not even knowing I'd dialed. "Can you pop over?"

Chapter 15

Sunday morning brunch at the Duchess was a tradition, and like every Sunday, I crawled out of my hangover, thinking I was late for it, before remembering it was a tradition to which I was no longer invited. The night before was as blurry as the night before that. His name was Chad, I think, and he'd been hot, but he'd wanted a top, and my coke-dick was having none of that. After all, like Jesse always said, two bottoms don't make a top (but two bottoms do make a top happy). Instead, it had been Sean Cody boys and frantic and furious masturbation until I came down and passed out.

I lay there in bed, the noonday sun beating through my window. I pulled the pillow over my face, trying to block out the light. My whole body was dried out and sore. Two days of being too dazed, and I was a wreck. Grunting, I sat up and caught my reflection in the mirror on my dresser.

I didn't even recognize myself.

I started to cry.

At first it was just a trickle, but the harder I stared at the face in the mirror, the more the tears streamed down my face. This had to stop. Maybe I had fucked everything up, but I could still make things right again. Maybe not easily, but I could put my life together again, right? Why should I let Nathan win like this? He had wanted to prove gay people couldn't get their happy-ever-after. I was proving him right.

"No more!" The sound of my voice in the quiet apartment startled me (and sent Griffin bolting from the room). "That's it! I'm really done!"

I stormed into the living room, opened up the drawer in the coffee table. There was the razor and mirror, coated in powder, half a line still left from last night. It called to me. "Do me," it said. "Sniff me." The pain of the hangover would go away, the pain of the feelings would go away. All I had to do was bend down and breathe it in.

"No!" I picked up the mirror and smashed it to the ground. Griffin peered out at me from his cat condo. Half-crying, half-laughing, I started to clean it up, thinking this was the first step to cleaning everything else up. With Dinah. With Brandon and the twins. With Aaron and Steven. I could make things better. I *would* make things better.

A knock at my door broke me from my train of thought. "Alex, you there? Open up." It was Walter's voice, hardly high on my list of people to see, but maybe it was a start.

"Just a second," I said, dumping the dustpan of broken mirror into the garbage.

"You okay?"

The urgency in his voice was almost comical. I was far from okay, but I was going to be. Why was he so worried? Just from the scene I caused at Wonderland Friday? Wiping my face dry from tears, I said as I opened the door, "Yeah, I'm fine, why do you ask?"

"Well, this," he said, gesturing at the wall. "I can't believe someone did it again."

"What are you talking about?" I stepped out into the hall and there, sprayed across my door in green paint, was FAGGOT.

It was a punch in the gut. I grabbed hold of Walter and slumped against the wall. I remembered so clearly coming home to see *faggot whore* painted in much the same way. That had been Allan, at Nathan's behest, right after I hooked up with Aaron at White Night. Was this Allan again? Why?

"Why?" I asked Walter, and started to cry again.

"You didn't know?"

"No, I haven't been out of my apartment since Friday. When . . . How long . . . ?"

"It wasn't there last night when I got home from the gym. Had to have happened overnight."

Faggot. Nathan's voice echoed in my head. It couldn't be . . . he couldn't have . . . He was locked up. He was gone. It was over.

But there it was. Again. *Faggot. Faggot. Faggot.* Why had I tossed away that coke? I could sure use some of it now.

"I'm sorry," Walter said, and I realized he'd been talking the whole time. "Should we call the police?"

No one ever did anything. At the end of the day, the only person you can count on is yourself. "Why? They're just going to write a report. There's no cameras on the building. It's just vandalism, they'll say. A mean prank. They won't do anything."

Could it have been Allan? It's the kind of sick thing that little fuckwad of a twink would do. He'd done it before. But why now? Why after all these months? But the more I stared at the word, the more it seemed exactly the same as the one before. The way it was sprayed there, the same. The hate behind the paint, the same. That twisted little druggie would think it was funny, messing with me after so long.

But where was he? He wouldn't be hanging around Wonderland anymore, that's for sure. Brandon would kill him. Where did all those boys go, when they were done with Brandon and wanting to avoid his raging drama? Wonderland was the club. There was nowhere else like it. Sure, there were places like the Hole, but that wasn't for kids. They wanted to dance and do their drugs, not cruise and fuck.

Brandon would know. Even though he hated them all when it was done, he was the kind of guy who would keep track of them. Stalk their Facebooks, and catfish them on Grindr, and do whatever he had to do to make sure they never forgot that they dared mess with Brandon Sweet. Brandon Sweet sure wasn't sweet, when it was all over.

Would he tell me? Would he even talk to me? Could I even talk to him? Only one way to find out, I guessed.

"Alex?"

"Thanks for checking on me, Walter, I appreciate it. I . . . I gotta go." I half-smiled at the neighbor I used to call the Walrus and went back inside. Things did indeed change. Hell, he'd known it was Allan who sprayed my door before (*faggot whore faggot whore faggot whore*), but he'd told me it was Aaron, all for the chance to suck some dick. He'd made amends though, or tried to anyway. And there was something to be said for that.

And maybe, there was something to be learned from that, too.

Chapter 16

Sitting on the couch, I stroked Griffin with one hand and stared at Brandon's name and number on my iPhone. Brandon who was all abs and ass. Brandon whose little twink du jour Allan had done Nathan's dirty work for him, fucking with my head and my life, and who had shown absolutely no remorse about it. Brandon who had punched me hard when he thought I'd hit on Allan. Brandon who had hit on me that same weekend. Brandon who I'd punched That Friday Night when things went wrong.

My finger hovered above the CALL icon. Taking a deep breath, I hit it, my hand trembling. It rang and then he answered. "Hello."

"Hey," I said. It was noisy in the background. Of course. He was still at brunch at the Duchess. With everyone.

"What's up, Alex?" The way he said my name, I could tell he was letting everyone know who was on the phone. I could almost see their faces.

"Sorry to bother you at brunch, but I need to talk to you. Can you come over after?"

"What's this about, Alex?"

"Please, Brandon. In person is better."

"Are you high?"

Ouch. That hurt. It was fair, but it hurt. Not that he was a saint, but it hurt. "No, and it's important. You know I wouldn't have called unless it was."

He sighed. "Just a sec." He had clearly put the phone down to talk to someone. I strained to hear, but couldn't make out what he was saying. "I'll be there in an hour or so. We just started brunch."

"Thank you, Brandon."

"Yah. See you." He hung up.

I deserved his coldness. I knew that. Brandon had definitely been on the receiving end of a few Drunk Alex texts. They all had. And now they were sitting there, sipping their mimosas and wondering what I could possibly have to talk to Brandon about. I wondered if they'd even care, if they knew about the graffiti (*faggot faggot faggot*). Had I used up all their sympathy? Why was I the one who was such a mess, they'd say as they said before, when it was Steven who'd been kidnapped, Steven who'd been beaten and tortured, Steven who'd been cheated on and lied to and betrayed by me? Nathan was from my past. It was to get to me that he'd done what he'd done. Steven was innocent and caught in the crossfire.

I stared at the wall, scratching Griffin behind the ears. Could it be Nathan? Was he paying Allan to do this again? Or was Allan on his own, doing it just for shits and giggles? Before, it had been for cash, which he'd used for drugs, but now, who knew? Maybe he'd been high and thought it would be funny. Maybe he knew how badly it had affected me before; Brandon would have told him, for sure. Sure, the words were different, the writing was different, the color was different, no *whore* this time, just a *faggot* (*faggot faggot faggot*), but it was the *faggot* that hurt.

The buzzer buzzed. Had it been an hour already? Sure enough, it was Brandon, and I felt my heart sink into my feet as I waited for him to catch the elevator up. What would he say? Would he yell? Would he condemn me for my actions and scream at me for my choices, and leave without even hearing what I needed to ask him? Did he hate me? Surely, they all must. All they had given me, all they had seen me through, and I threw it all away? I'd hate me, if I were them.

I waited for the knock at my door, dreading, dreading, dreading. I was just heading over to the door when it opened. Brandon ran in, and wrapped his arms around me, and all he said was, "Are you okay?"

I fell to the floor in his arms and started to cry again.

Chapter 17

How long I cried I don't know, but all Brandon did was hold me, petting my hair, rocking me back and forth as it all came out. All the guilt and regret and self-loathing, and all the fear that that *faggot* brought back.

"Why me?" he asked. "Why did you call me?"

"It was Allan before," I said, "and I thought maybe it was him again. Do you know where he is?"

"I haven't seen him since everything happened. He knows I would kill him if he set foot in my bar."

"So you have no idea where he'd be?"

"Well . . ." He blushed. "No, that's not entirely true. I keep tabs on the little fucker. I keep tabs on *all* the little fuckers."

"Where is he hanging out these days? I need to know if this was him again."

"Alex, why, though? Why would it be him?"

"He did it before, Brandon. This is exactly the same."

"Well, he's got to be hanging out at Boyz."

"What the fuck is Boyz?"

"The new flash-in-the-pan club. Where have you been hiding? Oh wait, never mind. Yah, it's been open a couple months now. It won't last. Better clubs have tried. Nothing beats Wonderland."

"But that's where he goes now?"

"It's got to be. That's where all those druggy little kids are hanging out. It's basically rent boys."

"Where is it? I'm going to find him."

"Okay, slow down, mister. First, you need to shower and change. You're a mess. It's early still, but they have a tea dance on Sundays, and I bet Allan will be working the room. We'll go in a bit."

"We?"

"Of course. A) I'm not letting you go by yourself, and B) if you're going to squash that little loser, I want to be there for it." He hugged me hard, and it was almost enough to make me tear up again. "Shower! Go!"

I laughed and went to get ready.

When I got out of the shower and was dressed, I walked into the kitchen to find Brandon stirring a pot of soup and making sandwiches. "What . . ."

"I figured you hadn't eaten. Hope you don't mind, but I thought you should get a little something in you."

"Brandon, I don't know what to say . . . I can't believe you."

"Just eat, Alex. Eat and listen." I sat down at the table and started into the lunch he'd made. "We all love you, mister. Yeah, you fucked up and pissed us all off, but we all love you. We're worried about you. I mean, don't get me wrong, I like my partying as much as the next gay, but you're out of control."

"I know. I . . ."

"No talking. Just eat. The other guys, they don't do the drugs thing at all. They don't understand it. I do. I like partaking. It's fun when you're out at the club, and having a good time. But you, you're doing it when you're by yourself. You're not doing it for fun. You're doing it to punish yourself, and that needs to stop. You didn't do anything that bad."

"I . . ."

"Just think about it, Alex. We're worried. If you have a problem, we will be there for you. I talked to the twins while you were in the shower. Well, I talked to Colton. Jesse's still hurt. You need to apologize for cutting him off. He might act all tough, like all he cares about is dancing and dick, but he's a softy. You know that. But the point is, they're here for you. We all are."

"What about Steven?"

"I didn't call him. That's between you guys. And I'm not gonna lie. He's mad, and very hurt."

The food was good, but the words were a bit harder to swallow. I knew they were true, but hearing them, they were punches in the gut, and my instinct was to hide. To call the Caterpillar, order in some white powder happiness, and fly high and numb. And the *faggot* on my door just added to my need for numbness.

But no, I couldn't do that. I wouldn't do that. That's all I had been doing for too long now. "I hear what you're saying, Brandon, and I'll try to make things better. I promise."

"Good boy, Alex. All done?"

I looked down, and sure enough, I'd eaten it all. Had I eaten yesterday? Maybe. Maybe not. "It was great, thank you."

"Okay, let's go see if we can't find Fucknuts."

Brandon held my hand as we left. "I don't think it was him, honestly though. What's in it for him? That little piece of shit is only out for himself."

"I thought that too, but I just don't know what else to do. And I have to do something."

"Something other than get high?"

"Stay out of my head," I said, with a smile. He smiled back.

It had been a long time since I had smiled with a friend. Whatever Allan's reason for the graffiti, I had to be grateful to him for opening the door to that.

Chapter 18

Wonderland was glamour. It was decadent and magical and you felt at home when you walked in, if your home was filled with spinning disco balls and lasers, hot shirtless men, sickening beats, and cheap, flowing booze.

Boyz was anything but glamorous. The music was distorted, the lighting was sad, and the men were anything but hot. The small bar was filled with old guys nursing their beer, as a pair of tragic little go-go boys danced on a small stage against the wall. Some men were watching, but most seemed indifferent.

Of course, I told myself, it is a Sunday afternoon.

"Wow, this is pretty sad," Brandon said. "I haven't been here during the day before, but wow."

"Why would you ever come here?"

"Oh, it's not always this tragic. Thursdays, they have a go-go contest. You'd be amazed by the boys that will take off their clothes for a few hundred dollars prize. And let's be honest. I can land for free what most of these sad trolls have to pay for."

We went up to the bar. "Want a drink?" Brandon asked.

Yes, absolutely, 100 percent. "No, I'm good. Maybe a water."

"Good call." He ordered us two bottles of water, and when the bartender came back with them, asked him, "Hey, I'm looking for a dancer friend of mine. Floppy bangs. Nice blue-green eyes. Huge dick."

"Allan?"

"You know him then?" Brandon said with a laugh.

"Oh, I know him, all right. He's not here yet, but will be along shortly. He's dancing tonight."

"What time?"

"Half an hour maybe?"

"Thanks, doll."

Brandon led me to a corner by the stage, obscured in shadow, perfect for us seeing him before he saw us. We sat there and drank our waters and talked about nothing in particular. The day-to-day minutiae of our lives these past months. Since I'd last seen him, there'd been a Kyle and a Steve, and he was now focused on the new Wonderland porter, Travis. As he regaled me with stories of his love life, he showed me pics of the boys on his iPhone, each one definitely Brandon's type, thin as a rail, smooth-bodied, and young. Not one stirred anything resembling lust in me. They were cute, but so young.

The boys on the stage were young, too, but not so cute. What did it take to lead someone here, dancing for dollars, being pawed at by random men? Surely the dollar bills stuffed in the PUMP! undies they wore couldn't justify it. And why would Allan be doing it? The kid was a fuckup and a total sociopath, but he was hot. Soulless, but hot. And who was I to judge? I had surely let enough random men paw me. At least these kids were making a few bucks at it.

The song that was playing ended, and the boys disappeared offstage. The men who were watching turned back to their tables and their drinks, and the bartender, skinny with a goatee as opposed to Wonderland's clean-shaven, well-toned clones, took the downtime to do a round of cleaning and serving on the floor.

"You guys want another?" he asked as he spun by. "Allan's in the back, he should be out soon."

"Gin cran please," I said without thinking.

"Make that two," Brandon said, and I felt his hand squeeze my knee under the table.

"So what do we do?" I asked. "Wait for him to finish dancing and surprise him? If he's guilty, he's going to bolt as soon as he sees us."

"Good point. Wait here."

Without explaining, Brandon left me alone to sit there and stare at the empty stage. The bartender brought our drinks, and I paid, and I stared into mine. Now that it was there, I wasn't sure I wanted it. After all, I'd been drinking a lot. Maybe it was time for a break. I swirled it around in the glass, and tried not to hear Nathan's voice in my head (*faggot faggot faggot*). Better Nathan's voice than Taylor's though.

Taylor. There was a voice to drive me to drink. My leg twitched.

The cran looked red and the gin smelled sweet. Maybe one sip wouldn't be so bad. My lips were touching the straw when Brandon showed back up with a dark-haired kid.

"Alex, this is James, he's one of the dancers."

I put down my drink and shook James's hand. I didn't need the drink that badly. Didn't need a fix-up with a go-go boy either, if that's where this was going, though. "Nice to meet you."

"You too. Brandon says you're here for Allan?"

"Well, in a matter of speaking . . ."

"They all come for Allan. Frankly, I don't see what the big deal is. Lots of other guys have big dicks, and they're not all crazy."

"Not an Allan fan, I take it?"

"Not at all, and not just because he blew the manager to get prime stage time. He's a liar and a thief."

"Well," Brandon said, "we need to have a little chat with Allan. There somewhere he can't see us until it's too late, and somewhere he can't get away from us?"

"Rip you guys off too?"

"You could say that, yes," Brandon said, and I suddenly had a new respect for my friend. This was a far more calculated approach than the screams-and-fists I expected.

"I can take you to our green room," James said. "He'll go back there when he's done. There's only the one door." He paused and looked at Brandon, then myself, appraisingly. "Maybe we can even find something to do while we wait . . ."

Brandon put his arm around the kid. "Maybe," he said, with that flirty Brandon smile I'd seen unleashed on so many unsuspecting people at Wonderland. "Can you show us where to wait, though?"

"Yeah, come with me."

I deliberately left my drink on the table as James took us backstage and down a hall filled with boxes of empties and reeking of stale booze.

"Wait here," James said, pointing to a shadowed recess. "I'm going to go see if Allan's still there." He gestured with his head to a green door.

"I am actually nervous about seeing him," Brandon said.

"Really, Brandon? It's me who should be nervous."

"Well, I suppose we both have a bit of just cause. He fucked with your life as much as he did my heart."

The "relationship" had been a week, if that, over before it began. How was that fucking with your heart? Heart? No. Ass? Yes. That's what I thought, but I just smiled reassuringly and squeezed his shoulder. The thought of seeing Allan again was working havoc on my stomach, and I kept thinking about the full gin and cran just sitting there, waiting for me, calling for me. I could call the Caterpillar, too, make the Sunday into a snow day. I could go home and forget about Allan and *faggot* and what that word on my door, again, might mean, for a life that was already about as unraveled as it could get.

I almost had myself convinced to go home when the green door opened and Allan ran down the hall, right past us, oblivious of course, in his Allan way, to anything that wasn't immediately in front of him or didn't concern him directly. He'd shaved his head since last I saw him, and it didn't at all suit him.

James came back for us. "Allan's on. He'll be out there for half an hour. Why don't we go to the green room and see if we can't entertain ourselves?" His grin was crooked, and his desperation obvious, but Brandon took him by the hand and we followed him into the green room, which was anything but. It was a dingy hole in the wall, with a clothes rack, a few stools, a couch, and a floor-to-ceiling mirror that ran the length of one wall.

"Have a seat," James said. "So, tell me what that fucker did to you guys?"

I couldn't unload myself to this stranger, but luckily, Brandon jumped to my rescue again, with a story he pulled out of thin air, about a one-night stand gone sour, about waking to a stolen wallet and iPhone. I closed my eyes as Brandon talked, and tried to lose myself in the blackness. I was on the edge. My whole body screamed for me to give it something.

Was I that lost to the addiction?

How long I stayed in my own head I don't know, but the door opening and closing pulled me back to the room.

"James went back to the bar," Brandon said, seeing me jump. "He says Allan should be done with his first set right away." He looked at me. "Are you okay, Alex?"

My lip quivered. "No, Brandon, I'm really not." Suddenly, my eyes were filled with tears and I collapsed onto his shoulder. He wrapped his arms around me and squeezed so hard, and I couldn't help it. I started to cry, big ugly sobs that left me gasping for air.

"You're gonna be okay, Alex. It's all going to be okay."

The door opened. "What the . . ." It was Allan's voice, and I barely had time to turn my head to see him before Brandon was pushing me aside and leaping across the room. He grabbed Allan by the shirt and threw him into the center of the room, then slammed the door. "What the fuck do you faggots want?"

I lunged at him. Down he went to the ground, me on top of him, and my hands were tight on his shoulders as I slammed him into the cheap carpet over and over and over. "Why did you do it? Why did you do it? Why did you do it?"

"Alex!" Brandon called out. "Enough!" He pulled me to my feet, my body vibrating.

"What the fuck, both of you? I'm calling the cops. You can't fucking come in here and assault me." He got up from the ground and headed to the door.

"Just tell us why you did it, Allan," Brandon said. "We know it was you." Brandon was in front of the door, no way the kid was getting out.

"Did what? What the fuck are you talking about? I haven't even thought of either of you two losers in months."

"You spray-painted my door again, you little shit. Why? Just to fuck with my head? There wasn't any money in it for you this time."

"Look, dude, I haven't been anywhere near your shit-hole apartment."

"You're lying!"

"Why would I lie? I have better things to do than waste time with you two."

Before, when cornered, he'd showed such bravado. This time, his repeated denial had me doubting myself. Maybe it wasn't him. But if not, who? "But you called us faggots just now," I said, "just like you wrote on my door."

"You're this upset over a stupid word on your door? Jesus Christ, you're pathetic. It's just a word, and we are."

"What?"

"What do you mean?"

"We are what?"

"Faggots," Allan said. "It's just a word, it can't hurt you."

Could this sketchy kid actually be making some sense? I fell back onto the couch, and Brandon sat down next to me. Allan stood there, sneering at us, rubbing the back of his head where I'd driven it into the ground.

"It's just a word," he said. "Now get the fuck out of here before I call the cops on you."

Brandon pulled me toward the door. As I went by Allan, I yanked myself free and took him by the shoulders. "Do you swear it wasn't you?"

"Shut the fuck up."

"Just promise me. Please."

He looked at me, and almost, his face seemed to soften. "It wasn't me." I believed him. "Go."

Brandon pulled me out into the hall and we were both looking back at Allan as he closed the door on us. If it wasn't Allan, then who could it have been?

Chapter 19

We walked down the hall in silence, and out in the lounge, James was dancing onstage. The room was busier, but I barely noticed. "Do you want to stay for a drink?" Brandon asked.

"You know, I actually don't." I was amazed, but it was true.

Brandon looked crestfallen though. "Oh, not because I'm not enjoying hanging out. I just don't want a drink, for the first time in a long time."

"That's good," he said, with a smile, and he squeezed my hand. "Let me take you home then."

We didn't say much in the car on the way back to my place from Boyz. What was there to say? The afternoon had been a waste really, and the graffiti on my door (*faggot faggot faggot*) was still a mystery. Who could have done it, and why? Maybe it was just a harmless prank. Maybe it was just a word, like Allan said.

I remembered a time when I used to say it was just a word too. That was me putting on a brave face to Dinah, to the world. I was made of steel, and their hate couldn't hurt me. But it always did, deep down, and last year, when Nathan paid Allan to write it on my door, it all came back. Even if it was just a word, who said words didn't have power? Faggot. Nigger. Cunt. Retard. Words I couldn't even think without flinching on the inside. Words had power. Words hurt.

But why would anyone want to hurt me when I was already so ripped apart?

"What are you thinking?" Brandon asked, pulling me out of my head again.

I smiled at him. "Right now, thinking that even if it wasn't Allan, even if I still have no idea who put it there, I'm glad it made me call you. Thank you, Brandon, for everything today. You're a good friend."

He pulled up outside my apartment building. "I love you, Alex," he said. "We all love you."

I could feel the tears welling up inside me again. "Do you wanna come up?"

"I should really get ready for work," he said.

"Oh, okay." I slumped a bit. Suddenly, I didn't want to be in that apartment by myself. I knew I'd cave. I knew I'd call the Caterpillar.

"Are you okay, Alex?"

I let out a deep breath. "I will be." I leaned over and hugged him, and then quickly got out of the car before I started to cry. I didn't look back as I heard Brandon drive off. My hands shook as I took out my keys. I could barely get them into the lock.

I would go upstairs. I would see it on my door. *Faggot faggot faggot.* I would be alone. I would know those words surrounded me. I would sit there on my couch with my phone in my hand and those words leaping from the wall into my brain. I would be alone, but I would call him. He would come over, and I would be happy and high and free, and I would hate myself. But I would be free.

Suddenly, I heard the squealing of brakes behind me, and I turned to see Brandon pulling a U-turn and peeling back up to the curb. He got out and smiled. "I called in sick. I think I need some Alex time."

A fat tear rolled down my cheek. This was a much better high, and even without the Caterpillar, right then I felt free.

We ordered in pizza. We watched bad movies. We laughed.

I missed laughing. I hadn't laughed with a friend in so long.

I forgot about Nathan, and Allan, and Steven, and Aaron. I forgot about the Caterpillar and his flowing cocaine. I forgot about the Hole and its empty sex. I forgot about *faggot.*

I glanced over at the clock and it was after midnight. The night had flown by. "Wow, it's late," I said.

"Not for a bartender," Brandon said, and I was suddenly very aware of those Brandon dimples. He was lounging on the couch, and his shirt was up, and I could catch a hint of those Brandon abs. "But it's a work night for you," he went on. "I should go." He stood up, and my heart lurched.

"Don't," I said, and I stood up to meet him, grabbing him by his hand, our faces inches apart.

"Alex, I . . ."

His breath was sweet and warm, and his lips were dry as I pressed mine against his. Our lips quivered against each other, but as I opened my mouth to invite him in more, he pushed me away.

"No, Alex, this isn't smart."

"It feels good."

"Yeah, it does."

"What's wrong then? We're both single, we're both hot."

"Alex, you know this isn't a good idea."

I took his hand and put it on my dick, and flexed my hard-on for him. "It feels like a good idea."

"It's not though. I should go."

He grabbed his jacket off the chair and put it on. "Don't go!"

"Alex . . ."

"Just stay, please. We don't need to fuck. I . . . I just don't want to be by myself tonight."

He looked at me and I looked back, and I could feel the desperation and the urgency and the patheticness leaking from my eyes into his. He took off his jacket. "Nothing's going to happen."

"I just don't want to sleep alone." I felt more naked with that admission than I would have been from any sex anyway.

Brandon was seeing every part of me that I had tried to keep hidden. And as we sat back down on the couch, as I curled up next to him and he put his arm around me, I felt a warmth spread through me.

Not just free. I was happy.

Chapter 20

I don't know when Brandon left, but when I woke up, I was alone. The clock read quarter after four, and I didn't even remember falling asleep. Flashes of what could have happened between me and Brandon filled my head as I left the couch and crawled into bed. There were a couple hours before I had to get up for work still, and even if I'd been sober the night before, I needed my beauty sleep.

My head had no sooner hit the pillow than I woke again, or at least, the waking you do inside a dream. *It was slow motion, Brandon behind the bar, all abs and ass and dimpled smile, unleashing his charm on every unsuspecting boy who walked up. All the while, he held eye contact tight with me, as the boys crawled over the bar, almost literally climbing him like he was a pole. (And what a pole, I thought, as the boys peeled off his undies and he stood there, naked and glorious like the dawn.)*

"I thought you loved me," Steven said, appearing to my right.

"I thought you loved me," Aaron said, appearing to my left.

There was a tap on my shoulder and I turned around. It was the Caterpillar, holding out a Baggie of cocaine. "I thought you loved this." I reached out for the coke.

"Decision made then," Aaron said, walking away.

"Hope it makes you happy," Steven said, walking away.

"That was easy," the Caterpillar said, disappearing off into the crowd, passing by Jesse and Colton and Dinah, all of whom stared at me with colorless eyes.

"You don't need that, Alex." It was Brandon, and he reached over my shoulder as I turned around and took the drugs away. But he didn't throw them out, he poured it out on the bar, and his bevy of boys flocked to it, and he expanded into immensity behind them, so that

each ab was the size of my head, and the chiseled spaces between them were canyons that the boys, all coked up and energetic now, disappeared into.

"Pathetic."

I turned around, but no one was there, just eyeless, faceless people in a crowd.

"Who said that?"

"Me."

"Where are you?"

I spun around in a circle, but it was just the eyeless and the faceless all around me. Brandon and the bar were gone and as far as I could see were mutant freaks with no eyes and sewn-together lips.

"Faggot."

"Come out!"

"You came out. All you faggots. Faggot. Faggot. Faggot."

"Stop it!"

I ran into the crowd, trying to follow the sound of the voice. Suddenly, I was on the edge of a cliff, barely stopping myself from going over. As I skidded to a halt, pebbles fell down to where surf broke on giant rocks.

"You're so pathetic, you might as well jump."

I turned around and out of the crowd of mutants on the cliff emerged Nathan, his blond hair mussed and his face covered in blood just like when he was lying on the floor. He reached out for me. "You won't be needing this." He took the gun from my hand.

"What do you want, Nathan?"

"What I've always wanted, faggot. To see you pay."

"I didn't do anything to you! It wasn't me!"

"You're all the same. You. My dad. His friends. Your precious little fiancé. Taylor."

"Why are you so obsessed with us?"

"Because you're all sick, and it's my job to end you." He stepped toward me. "One at a time!" He pushed me off the cliff and as I fell toward the rocks below, he leaned over the cliff, his face inflating like Brandon's abs, and he laughed and he laughed and the blood dripped down . . .

And I woke up.

Chapter 21

Nathan.

The clock read seven. I was late getting up for work, but they were somewhat getting used to that. I hurried to shower and shave and dress, but all the while, I couldn't shake the dream.

Nathan.

We had known each other all our lives. We'd been in kindergarten together. His family lived across the street from mine for five years. We played together every day growing up. We were almost like brothers. But then adolescence kicked in and things were different. I was different. I definitely looked at him differently.

At night, his was the face in my head when I'd furtively jerk off, and the teenage shame at jerking off was exacerbated by the surety that it wasn't supposed to be a guy's face in my head. Especially not my best friend's.

Nathan.

We were both fifteen. We were alone in his room, studying. We had to look something up on the computer.

"Want to watch some porn?" he asked me. "My parents don't have anything blocked."

I just nodded. I didn't know what else to say.

A few clicks later, and the screen was full of tits, and the girl was fingering herself. Nathan's eyes were locked on the screen. My eyes kept darting from the computer to his crotch, and the more he rubbed himself, the more I watched him. I was rock hard, and my best friend was beautiful and blond and slim and smooth and I could tell he was just as hard. My hand was suddenly on his thigh.

"Dude, what are you doing?" He jerked away as I jumped to my feet. "What are you, some kind of faggot? Get out of my room!"

I ran from his house, and behind me, I could hear him still calling, "Faggot! Faggot! Faggot!"

That was before Taylor. After I met Taylor, everything was different. First love. When I touched Taylor, Taylor touched me back. And everything was wonderful, and the looks that Nathan would give me at school, the way he would shove us or call us faggot, it didn't matter, and once we stopped reacting, he stopped. But when Taylor's dad found out, Taylor's dad's "Faggot! Faggot! Faggot!" was way, way worse than anything Nathan had ever said.

After Taylor killed himself, I never spoke to Nathan again, and after high school ended, I never thought of Nathan again. Until the night I found Steven. Nathan had stalked me, kidnapped the man I loved, held him hostage, and led me on a wild chase to get Steven back. And he would have killed both of us if I hadn't broken free and shot him with his own gun.

Nathan. He was in jail, and not getting out anytime soon. He couldn't have had anything to do with this newest graffiti. Maybe I just needed to forget about it. Maybe I just needed to get it painted over (again! Mr. Carroll would love me!). It was just a word, after all.

Taylor dying. That hurt.

Steven getting kidnapped and tortured. That hurt.

Seeing Steven with Aaron. That hurt.

Losing all my friends. Sitting at home by myself. Drowning in booze and blow and nameless boys. That hurt.

Faggot? It's just a word.

Chapter 22

I called Mr. Carroll from work. He was easily one of the best landlords I'd ever met, and he promised to have the wall and door painted over before I got home. I wouldn't let it affect me.

I texted Brandon, too, thanking him for being a friend, and adding that as hot as he was, I was glad he had stopped things from progressing. He'd hit on me before, but he was right. We were friends. And sex couldn't fill the void any more than drugs or booze.

Besides, what good were two bottoms together? Not that I was a total bottom, but lately, I couldn't bring myself to top. Getting fucked hard, that's the only way I got off.

I was well into my day, and completely focused on the pile of paperwork in front of me, when my phone rang. It was Colton: **Brandon told me what happened. Are you okay?**

I wanted to text back more. I wanted to say I was sorry for what I'd done, what I'd said. To say I was sorry for being an all-around mess. To say ignoring them for all these months was a beyond douchey thing to do.

All I wrote was, **yes.**

And then, **thanks.**

And then, **how are you?**

And then, **I miss you. Colton, I'm sorry for being such a screwup.**

Whoa, slow down there. We're good.

Tell Jesse.

Tell Jesse yourself. We're good, you and me. You and him, that's another story. You hurt him, Alex. You hurt all of us, but really, you hurt him.

I know. I'm sorry.

Sorry's just a word, he wrote back.

True, I thought. Just like *faggot.* Words didn't mean anything. How could I show them that I meant it? What big gesture did I need to make?

It's the best I can do right now.

It's a start, and like I said it's good enough for me.

I stared at the phone, hoping he had more to say, hoping he knew the magic words I needed to say to fix everything. But it sat there. And I sat there watching it, and the minutes passed, and then it was home time, and there were no magic answers.

I was just one sorry faggot.

But, on the way home, I realized I was one sorry faggot who had gone a full day without cocaine or alcohol, and maybe that wasn't much of an accomplishment for a lot of people, but it was for me. And I wanted to share it with someone.

And that someone was Steven.

It was still Steven. All the random dick in me, kissing Brandon, even all the sexcapades with Aaron and the twins months ago, none of that meant anything. I loved Steven.

I'm going to call him, I decided. *Maybe not tonight, but soon.*

I parked and headed into my building. Mr. Carroll was in the lobby.

"I got it done," he said. "Do you know when it happened?"

"It had to have been Saturday night. It wasn't there Friday but Walter told me about it yesterday morning."

"Any idea who?"

"My friend Brandon and I went and asked the freak who did it last time. He said it wasn't him, and I believed him. I am hoping it was just a random homophobic prick."

"Lots out there," Mr. C said, "and it seems like it's getting worse."

"It sure does, thanks for taking care of it for me." As we talked, I headed toward the mailboxes and unlocked mine.

"Anytime, it's my job, after all."

"I owe you."

"Your friend Jesse available yet?"

I laughed. "No, they're still together. They do do thirds, though."

He smiled. "I don't. Thanks anyway."

As I waited for the elevator, I flipped through the pile of mail. Bill. Flyer. Flyer. Occupant.

"Oh my God."

I slumped against the wall, and dropped everything I was holding. Who . . . How . . . Why . . .

"What is it?"

It was happening again. Something wicked my way was coming, and in my hand was proof.

A picture of Taylor, my beautiful, beautiful Taylor. And scrawled across it, *You Killed Me.*

"No, no, no, no, no." I ripped the picture into pieces and threw them as far away from me as I could, then I collapsed onto the floor and cried.

Chapter 23

He was sixteen going on seventeen when we met. His family had just moved and he was behind in class, and our teacher had asked me to help him with his math homework. Later, I wondered if Mrs. Whiting had known. We were both pretty obviously gay, and maybe she thought that was a way to make it easier on us.

Our first kiss was magic. Well, not our first kiss. Our first kiss, we were both laughing so hard, it didn't really work out. Our next kiss though, just moments later, when he looked at me with those big puppy-dog brown eyes, when I brushed away that big bang of his that always flopped over his face, it was pure magic. And I fell in love with him the moment our lips met.

From that first kiss, we became each other's world. Yes, Dinah was my best friend even back then, but Taylor was my everything. He knew all my secrets, I knew his. Together, we found the courage to ignore the Nathans of the world. And as we explored each other's bodies, we shared each other's hearts.

But then his mom walked in on us, and we were doing a lot more than math homework. The lights came on before we had time to pull away from each other, much less pull a blanket over us, and there was no denying what two boys in a naked 69 looked like. Her awkward apology was followed not too long later by his dad screaming out, "A fucking faggot? No son of mine!"

Taylor kissed me as I crawled out his window. That was the last time Taylor ever got to kiss me. The next day at school, he could barely see. He wouldn't even talk to me, but it was clear from the bruises on his beautiful, beautiful face that his dad had beat him up. That night, his mom wouldn't let me talk to him on the phone, and I was terrified what would happen to him, what would happen to us. I knew it was stupid but I ran over to his place in the middle of the night and threw rocks against his window until he opened it up.

"You can't be here, Alex!" he whispered at me.

"I had to know you're okay."

"I'm fine. Go."

"I don't believe you. Can I come in?"

"No!" His expression was terrified. "We can't hang out anymore."

"I love you, Taylor."

"Don't say stuff like that. It's wrong."

"No, it's not! It's real. Two hearts, one heart, remember?"

"You need to go, Alex. It's over."

"Just tell me you're okay."

"I'm going to be fine," he said. His terror had faded, and his face was just empty now. "Bye, Alex."

"I love you," I said again, to the closing window.

That was the last time I got to say that to him.

The next morning, he was dead. He had shot himself with his father's gun, and his beautiful face was gone forever. His beautiful heart was gone forever. He was gone forever.

Chapter 24

Somehow, I got back to my apartment. Somehow, I found my phone and made the call. Somehow, I made it through the twenty minutes it took for him to get there. Somehow, I buzzed him in. Somehow, I found the strength to find the cash and trade it, my money for his drugs. I cursed myself for smashing my mirror, but luckily, there was a backup on my wall. I ripped it off and cut out a fat line of the Caterpillar's finest.

There was a time and a place for sobriety. There was a time and a place for being on the wagon. That time was not now. That place was not here.

White fire filled my brain and it pushed away the image of his picture. *You killed me.* Had that sick twisted fucker Nathan actually sent me this from jail? Didn't they screen outgoing mail? Didn't they make it impossible for a monster to keep attacking his victim?

But no sooner did the cocaine rip through my brain than a wave of guilt swept over me. Why did I do it? No! I needed it! To be sent that picture . . . and no, not just sent that picture. It was loose among the rest. Someone had shoved it into my mailbox! Not Nathan sending me his venom from prison. Someone hand-delivering his poison.

More coke followed. Line after line ripping through me, and gin, beautiful gin, to wash it down. I cradled my skull in my hands and screamed out in pain and rage and frustration and guilt, and I shook with sobbing, and all I could see was Taylor's beautiful face and Nathan's hate-filled face and Steven's bruised and bleeding face and Jesse's hurt and disappointed face.

Maybe Nathan was right. Maybe Taylor was right. Maybe sorry faggots didn't deserve to live. It sure didn't seem possible that we could ever get that happy-ever-after. The writing was literally on the wall, and if a picture was worth a thousand words, even a ripped-up picture, then that was a thousand giant *faggots* demanding I pay, demanding I suffer.

And I was powerless, but not powderless. The face in the mirror as I leaned over it to cut my next line was a stranger, and it was a stranger who wanted to forget. And what I couldn't forget in gin and cocaine, I could forget in the pillow.

I fired up Grindr, and each window was an invitation to forget. My square was faceless, just my body, which wasn't as good as it once had been. Who had time for the gym when the world was falling apart? But I flipped through profiles, one after another after another, and there he was, a chiseled and smooth torso of a man, looking for a bottom.

What's up, I sent him, and added a picture of my ass.

I had barely inhaled the new line before he replied back. **Nice ass, bro**, and the dick pic he reciprocated with had my hole twitching.

I sent back my address, and poured out another gin. It burned going down. I stripped off as I waited for him to come, this faceless man with that impressive dick, and I cut out a couple more lines, in case he wanted to party before we played.

I waited, flipping through the other profiles in case he didn't show. They were never no-shows, though. The pic of my ass I sent out when I was looking to get plowed was a good picture. A really good picture. No horny top could say no, and I was flying high enough to believe my own hype. I was invincible and strong and there were no words and no pictures and no memories of Taylor inside this bubble.

Finally, the buzzer rang, and I let him in without a word. My dick was half hard at the thought of him inside me, and it twitched when he knocked at the door.

I opened the door, and there stood Allan.

"I thought I recognized the address," he said with a sneer.

A thousand thoughts collided inside my head. Of all the people on all the cruising apps, it was this sketchy ex-fuck of Brandon's who had helped Nathan torment me. But he did have a big dick, and the whole situation was fucked up enough to be extra satisfying.

I pulled him toward me and my mouth closed on his.

Chapter 25

My mouth was dry and my dick was hard, and he pushed me into the apartment.

"I always wondered what it would be like to fuck you," he said. "Not just fuck with you," he added, with that sneer.

"Don't talk," I said. "I just want to get fucked."

"What would Brandon say?"

"I said, don't talk!" I shoved my tongue in his mouth again to shut him up.

We fumbled our way to the couch, and he forced me to sit. He stood above me, and stripped off, and there it was, the body from the profile, the dick from my memory, and I dropped to my knees and went down on him, feeling it grow in my mouth. His hands tangled in my hair and he pulled me down, down, down until I was gagging on his growing meat.

It was wonderful.

I thought of Brandon and all the times he would have gone down on this cock, and I could see his abs flexing as he bent over to take it all in. My hand was on my dick, faster and more furious than any drag racing movie.

Allan groaned as I picked up speed on his dick, my hands squeezing his ass and pulling him even deeper into my face. "Slow down there, Alex, I'm going to make this good." He pulled my head off. "Mind if I have one?" He gestured with his head toward the coke.

"Go hard."

"Oh, I will," he said, and he leered at me. He bent down and sniffed up one of the lines as I licked his back down to his ass. Another night, I'd've buried myself balls deep in that ass, but I wanted to get fucked. I wanted to get fucked until I couldn't walk. I wanted to get fucked until I couldn't think.

"You go," he said, holding out the straw for me.

I took it from him, and inhaled the storm. As I pulled back, eyes closed, breathing in the white fire, his hand was on my ass, spreading my cheeks apart, his fingers seeking entrance. His spit hit my hole warm and wet, and then he pushed his way in, one finger, two. I grunted, arching my back, pushing back onto his hand.

I tossed him the bottle of lube I kept stashed under the couch for just such situations. "Get. In. Me. Now."

"Yah? You want it?"

"Yes." I looked back at him. "I want it."

"Beg for it."

"Please, Allan, please give it to me."

He slapped his dick against my ass. He was so hard. My whole body shivered. "Please, Allan."

"Say please again, you slutty little faggot."

I tensed. *Faggot faggot faggot.* But it was true. That's what I was, what I'd always been.

"Yah, I'm just a fag, and I want you in me now." I reached down, grabbed his lubed-up dick, guided it to my twitching hole. He slapped my hand away.

"My rules," he said. He pushed my head down into the couch. I could barely breathe. And then he was in me, and I stretched to accommodate him, and he slammed hard and fast, and I screamed.

It was wonderful.

Over and over and over he pounded into me, and with every thrust, I was driven farther into the couch. He was silent now, relentless, a fucking machine that existed only to ruin me. I moaned louder as his speed increased. My own dick lay forgotten between my legs, but this destruction was better than any orgasm. "Fuck me fuck me fuck me fuck me fuck me fuck me fuck me fuck me."

My heart was racing, from the exertion, from the coke, from the thoughts that kept eating away at the edges. My eyes were closed, and I could see Taylor, lying on his back, the first time I fucked him, so many years ago, and the way he would bite his lip to keep from crying out. I cried out louder. That was then, and we were young and new. Now, it didn't matter, and this dick was attached to a vile and sick man who was nothing like my Taylor. He filled me, and made me emptier.

He yanked my head back. "You like this, Alex? You like my cock in you?"

"Yes."

"Tell me you like it."

"I like it!"

"Tell me you love it."

"I love it. Fuck me! Harder, goddammit! Harder!"

He pulled out, and I gasped at the sudden vacancy. "On your back, faggot."

I rushed to comply, my hands holding my knees to my chest. He yanked me to the edge of the couch, lined up, and drove his cock mercilessly into me. His hands on my ankles bent me nearly in half and over and over and over again, he pounded against me. His head was thrown back, he wasn't seeing me any more than I was seeing him. I reached out, touching his face, and he opened his eyes. They were cold. He smiled, a smile that didn't reach those cold eyes.

Suddenly, he pulled out again, climbed on top of me, and shot all over my face. I jerked myself back to hardness as he unloaded hot and wet, wiping his cum from my face and using it as lube on myself. He wiped his dick on a throw pillow and started to get dressed, his eyes holding mine as I continued to frantically fuck my fist.

He leaned down and kissed me on the mouth, and I could taste his cum, and then he pulled my head down, and whispered in my ear, "Didja like that, faggot?"

I groaned and came.

I lay there and watched him walk out without another word. When the door closed behind him, I rolled onto my side, saw the coke-covered mirror, felt the semen drying on my skin, and started to cry.

Chapter 26

I was on fire.

No wait. That was just the sun, bright and blinding and basically peeling away my eyelids.

Gingerly, I opened one up and flinched. I was on the couch still, and there wasn't a part of me that didn't hurt. Bits and pieces of the night floated through the screaming corners of my mind, disjointed and blurry recollections of Allan fucking me, of the picture of Taylor, of lying there into the night, my heart racing from the drugs.

The clock on my wall said two. It clearly wasn't two in the morning. The sun outside was high.

The gin was spilled on the mirror. What a waste of perfectly good wake-me-up coke! Wait. What day was it?

Tuesday?

Fuck.

It hurt to walk but I moved around to look for my phone, and found it, kicked under the coffee table, slimy with lube. Griffin meowed, and it was like nails down the backs of my eyes.

"Shut up, cat," I said, but my own voice hurt just as much.

Three voice mails. Never good. Texts were fine. Actual phone calls meant trouble.

"What the fuck, Alex?! How could you? I spent the entire day helping you and then you invite him over and he fucks you? Are you fucking insane? I thought you were starting to get your shit together but clearly I was wrong. Lose my number. We are done!"

Of course. Allan of course had to brag to Brandon. It was a punch in the stomach. All the good that had happened on Sunday, it was all set back.

"Alex," the next one began. It was my boss. *"We've been trying to*

call you all morning. I don't know what's going on with you but this is too much of a common occurrence this past while. We will be sorry to lose you but it's just not working out anymore. No need to come in. We'll mail you your final check."

I slumped to the floor, and my mind raced, trying to think how many lates or absences there'd been the past few months. They added up. I started to laugh. Fired was just the icing on a shitty fucking life. I turned my phone off. There was no way I wanted to hear the third voice mail. After rock bottom, where else was there to go?

Griffin rubbed up against my face. I shoved him away. He meowed again. "Shut up, cat!"

I laughed even harder. It really was impossible to believe. Everything turned to dust in my hands. Relationships, jobs . . . everything. Even my past. That picture of Taylor, its taunt of *You killed me*. How was I supposed to move on, make things better, when everything kept pulling me back down? How was I supposed to get Nathan to stop?

I needed my Dinah.

Turning my phone back on, I called her, but of course, it went directly to voice mail. She, unlike me, was at work. She, unlike me, had a job. And a fiancé. And friends. And a life. I, unlike her, was just a sorry little faggot (*faggot faggot faggot*).

What the hell. Might as well face it all. I checked the third voice mail.

At first, I thought it was a hang-up, but then he spoke. I melted into tears at the sound of his voice. My Steven.

"Alex. We need to talk. I don't know what's going on, but clearly a lot. Brandon, Colton, Walter, Mr. Carroll, everyone has called me. At first, I didn't want to get involved. You'd made your choices, and the consequences were yours to deal with. But if you're really in trouble, I'm here. Call me if you need to."

I could barely see my phone through the tears. Even after all I'd said and done, he was reaching out. Oh God, what would he think when he heard about Allan? Or that I was fired? Did he know how bad things had truly gotten? Aside from the new stuff, like the picture of Taylor. Did he know how bad the drug use had gotten?

It had just cost me a job, and it had definitely cost me my dignity. Had I really let Allan fuck me? Allan? Of all people? And had he really made me orgasm with *faggot?* I hated that word. How could I have reacted that way? I just wanted things back like they were, before all this, before the kidnapping. When it was that practically perfect summer of me and Steven.

He was saying hello before I even realized I had called him back. The sound of his voice pulled only sobs from me.

"Alex?"

I couldn't talk.

"Are you okay?"

"No."

"I'll be right there."

The phone went dead, but suddenly, I felt alive again.

Chapter 27

When we escaped from Nathan, Steven and I were both convinced the worst was behind us. We had survived, Nathan was arrested. He confessed to it all, and we were free. Steven had my ring on his finger, and we were free.

But first, I had to tell him everything.

I had wanted to propose, of that I had no doubt. But still, a panic set in, and that panic led to me visiting Wonderland and getting some drugs from the Caterpillar, one last snowy night before settling down to a white-picket-fence happy ending. Those were the drugs he found, and that fight was bad. It ended with him saying he never wanted to see me again.

In grief and anger, I went back to Wonderland, and left there that night, drunk and high with a twin on each arm. That threesome with Jesse and Colton was a mistake, but Steven had to know. He had to forgive. They had always had a strange openness to their relationship that neither Steven nor I understood, and they hadn't thought twice about taking me home with them, whether Steven and I were together or not. The couple that played together, stayed together was their motto, and if it worked for them, it could work just as easily for us.

Except I woke up the next day feeling horribly guilty, but whenever I wanted to reach out to him and tell him, I remembered that he had said he wanted nothing to do with me. And so I said nothing. And that night, I saw him in his window with someone else, and I thought we were even Steven.

What if I had burst in on him that long ago Saturday? I would have caught him with Nathan, who was using Steven's grief and his own good looks to trick Steven, to capture him. Everything else would have been avoided if I had simply gone all Brandon on him right there, bursting in, in drama and rage. But no, I had chosen to wander away, and the next morning, Steven was missing.

Steven knew what Nathan was telling me to do. While I was waiting for the calls from this anonymous evil, Steven was subjected to Nathan's crazy rants 24/7. Steven heard all about what Nathan had suffered as a child, in incoherent ramblings mostly, but he pieced it together. And as Nathan set out to prove that gay people couldn't ever know true love, Steven held on to the idea that I would do whatever I needed to get him back.

Which for Nathan meant me going to White Night at the local bathhouse, having sex with a stranger, and then confessing my infidelity to Steven. All the while, Allan was helping Nathan along, keeping watch on what I was doing, messing with my life, all for the promise of a fat wad of cash.

Nathan hadn't been able to predict that that anonymous bathhouse fling he sent me out to would be anything but anonymous. Aaron showing up there that night changed everything. Our hookup served Nathan's purpose, but Aaron showing up in my life, after all our years together and those last two years apart, confused the hell out of me, and as Nathan's calls kept stringing me along, Aaron's presence in my life was familiar and comfortable, and old feelings floated to the surface.

I told Steven about the foursome that followed, and not even the fact that Allan had drugged me changed the fact that I was an essentially willing participant. Liquor and G and jealousy and dormant attraction led to that night with Aaron and the twins, and I had to accept ownership for what I had done. It wasn't easy, but I did it.

Even harder was telling Steven what happened next. When I found out the truth about Aaron, that he had quit his job, moved here, and been keeping tabs on me as the sensational Queen of Hearts at Wonderland, it only added to my confusion. That was a grand romantic gesture. It meant something. And so much had already happened, and I was still so unshaken in my love for Steven, that Aaron and I spent one last night together, and this time, there wasn't the excuse of a crazed kidnapper or being drugged. There was just that itch that needed scratching one last time. It wasn't a beginning; it was a good-bye.

And then I was able to find Steven, with help from Aaron and Brandon, and rescued him from Nathan, and the teary confessions that followed were forgiven, and Steven welcomed Aaron into our lives. And we were all friends, and everything was wonderful: Steven and Aaron and myself and Brandon and Jesse and Colton.

I never let myself think that every time Steven saw almost any of those people, he had to remember that I'd been with them.

I never let myself think about the fact that while I was running about, ostensibly waiting for clues or orders from the kidnapper, drinking at Wonderland, having all that confused and confusing sex, he was bound and beaten. Nathan would vanish for hours at a time, and then come back and harangue him about the evils of gays in general, and me in particular, how I betrayed him by touching him as horny teenagers. Steven suffered, and I partied.

I never let myself think of that. And Steven never indicated that he thought of it. It was as if the entire week never happened. I never commented when the engagement ring came off. Everything was eggshells and broken glass and fine lines. I was careful not to endanger the delicate equilibrium we were both so happy we had created.

Until That Friday Night.

Chapter 28

The buzzer rang and pulled me from my memories of That Friday Night. Since That Friday Night, I had hardly seen Steven, and when I had, it was angry at worst, awkward at best. Even when I hadn't seen him, it was drunken texts and phone calls. But now, he was here, for me, at my darkest.

And that had to count for something. That had to count for everything.

I buzzed him in and unlocked the door. I poured us both drinks. It didn't matter if it was the middle of a Tuesday afternoon. This could only be made better with alcohol. Alcohol was safety and numbness and protection. What did he already know? What would I tell him?

He knocked three times, each one ringing ominously in my head.

I opened the door and there he was, my Steven. He was wearing a white dress shirt, just like he was the day I first saw him, getting into his white Rabbit in the parking lot at the grocery store. It fit tighter than I remembered. Had he been working out? It looked good. Was it for Aaron? Dinah said there was nothing going on between them, but I knew what I'd seen. He looked good.

He looked really good, and it was a good that used to be mine.

"Can I come in?"

"Wha . . . oh . . . sure."

He passed by me, brushing against me. I could smell his cologne.

"Okay," he said, "tell me what's going on."

"Drink?" I asked, handing him the extra I'd made.

"This isn't a social call, Alex."

"I know." I sat down on the couch to stop my legs from trembling.

He sniffed and smiled. "What's up?" He took the drink and sat down next to me.

"What do you know?"

"I know about the graffiti on your door. Walter *and* Brandon *and* Mr. C called me to tell me. They're all really worried."

"That's sweet."

"Brandon says you went to see Allan with him though, and he says it wasn't him."

I wondered what else Brandon had said about Allan. Steven didn't seem mad, but would he get mad? We were over, and really, Allan was the least of my sins. "He said it wasn't."

"Do you believe him?"

"I actually do." In spite of how he'd acted when he was fucking me. In spite of his last whispered words.

"Maybe it was just a random hate crime."

"No, I don't think so."

"What else? That's not everything, is it?"

"No."

"Tell me, Alex."

I finished my drink and took a breath. "I got something in my mail."

"What?"

"It was a picture. Of Taylor."

"From high school Taylor?"

"No, Taylor Swift. Yes, from high school Taylor."

"Who would send you that?"

"Someone shoved it in there. It wasn't in an envelope."

"What aren't you saying?"

"Someone wrote on it. It said 'You killed me.' "

"What? Are you serious?"

I couldn't help the tears leaking out. "Yes."

And then his arms were around me, and the tears flowed.

"That's sick, Alex. I don't even know what to say." He pushed me back and took my face in his hands. They were soft against my cheeks. "Are you okay?"

"No, Steven, I'm really not. I'm pretty fucking far from okay."

"Do you have any idea who it could be?"

"It has to be Nathan."

"But from prison?"

"Who else?"

"I don't know, but we aren't going through this again." My heart soared at the *we.*

"What can we do?"

"We're going to see him in the morning. I have sick time coming. Can you call in?"

"Yeah, about that . . ."

"What?"

"I kinda got fired."

"Fired? Jesus, Alex, what's going on with you?"

"Things fell apart."

"Clearly."

"I miss you."

"Oh no, we aren't going there. I will go with you to confront Nathan. I will make sure you're okay. We aren't talking about *us.*"

"Sorry. Don't be mad."

"Mad? I'm not mad, Alex. I wasn't ever mad."

"What then?"

He laughed. "You're not doing this. I just said we aren't having this conversation. You always do this. You always just run over whatever I am saying and keep it where you want it to be." He shook his head, but he was smiling when he did it. "And there's only ever been one way to stop you."

And then he kissed me.

Chapter 29

Since That Friday Night, a lot of lips had touched mine. Grindr hookups; bathhouse flings; drunken, hot mess nights at the Hole. Lips from faceless men, men who were just means to an end, just dicks to my end.

Those kisses didn't make my body vibrate like Steven's did. It pushed away everything: getting fired, getting fucked, getting high, getting pictures. Everything fell apart, and it was just his lips on mine.

But then it popped into my head again, the image of them in bed. The image of them kissing. The image of them fucking. I pulled away, my body suddenly shaking.

"No," Steven said. "I know what you're thinking about. Don't."

He kissed me again, harder this time. I squeezed my eyes hard, pushing away the pictures, and I kissed him back. I lay down, pulling him down on top of me, my hands pulling up his shirt.

"Alex, I don't know if we should."

"You kissed me."

"I know, but just to stop you talking or thinking. I think we shouldn't."

"I think we should."

He held my arms down and looked in my face. "We aren't."

"We are." I strained to kiss him again.

"Brandon called me, Alex. I know what you did last night. I know *who* you did last night. We aren't having sex."

I pushed him off me. "Then why kiss me?"

"It felt right. And then it felt wrong. It was a mistake. I'm sorry."

"Maybe you being here is a mistake. Maybe you should go."

"I'm not leaving you alone, Alex."

"You really want to stay? You want to see what my life is like now?"

"Yes, I want to help you."

"Don't fucking patronize me." I slammed back the last of my gin. "That helps me." I opened up the drawer, pulled out the coke-covered mirror. "This helps."

"For fuck's sake, Alex. I don't want to see that."

"You said you did. You said you want to know what my life is like. This is my life now."

"It doesn't have to be."

"It does! You left me with nothing else!"

"No! You left yourself with nothing else."

"Steven, you were doing Aaron."

"That one time! With you! That was it! Never before and never since! I barely even talk to Aaron." He looked away.

"Did you finish?"

"What?"

"After I left that night. Did you guys finish?"

"What difference does it make now?"

"I want to know. I want to know if you were so upset by the fight that everything stopped, or if you guys just rolled over and kept fucking while I went to Wonderland, got fucked up, got into a fight with everyone. Was his dick in your ass while my life fell apart?"

"Yes, okay? Yes, he fucked me. You left! It was supposed to be with you. It was supposed to be for you! But you made it all about you and stormed off! Yes, he fucked me, just like he fucked you when I was tied to that chair. Is that what you wanted to hear, Alex? Is that what you wanted to know?"

We were standing now, and he was waving his arms. All the frustration and anger and self-loathing and jealousy and misery of the past six months came pouring out of my mouth in a huge scream and I threw myself at him, fists flying. He caught my arm in his hand as I punched at his face. He pushed me down to the ground. I kept struggling against him, my limbs flailing, but he'd been working out and I hadn't set foot in a gym in months. He had me pinned on the ground.

"Stop it!" he said. "Just stop it. Right fucking now."

"Get off me! Get off me!"

"Stop it!"

"Please, just get off me." I started crying. "I'm sorry, I'm sorry. I'm so sorry."

I pulled him on top of me and held him, our chests heaving against each other as we tried to catch our breath. “Everything fell apart. I let everything fall apart. You wouldn’t believe what I’ve done, Steven. I am so sorry. I made such a mess of everything. You must hate me.”

“Would I be here if I hated you, Alex?”

“Then it’s just pity. I’m just your pathetic ex whose life you’re here to fix.”

“You’re not pathetic, Alex. You’ve just been lost. But I’m here, and we’ll find you again.”

Chapter 30

We sat there on the couch, staring at each other. It was the calm after the storm. I replayed everything in my head. That had always been my problem, replaying everything over and over, how things went, how things could have gone, how things should have gone. Sometimes, I even ended up replacing the actual with the imagined. I knew I did that, and Steven knew I did that.

Five minutes passed, maybe ten. Then Steven grabbed the remote. "Want to watch a movie?"

I nodded, and he flipped through Video on Demand until we found something we both hadn't seen. We sat on opposite ends of the couch, watching it in silence. We were a commercial for perfect posture, sitting there so straight and rigid; I was nervous to even look at him, but by the end of the movie, we had both relaxed, sinking into the couch, our feet touching in the middle.

When the movie was over, I got up. "Are you hungry? I could cook something."

"Since when do you cook? You sit down. I'll cook something."

I smirked, and he smiled back. "Well, I can't do nothing while you cook."

"You could clean this up," he said, indicating the booze and blow and mess around the couch, from last night's sexcapade, from today's fight. "You can probably just throw this all out. You don't need it."

"I don't want to need it."

"You *don't* need it," he repeated, "but it's your choice."

He went into the kitchen and I stared into the mirror. He was right, I knew that. It was my choice. It was such an easy fix, though. It buffered me against all the bullshit, and if another confrontation was coming with Nathan, I needed all the buffer I could get. Unless . . .

could Steven be that buffer for me, this time? Could I face Nathan and get him to stop with this twisted game, with only Steven by my side and no alcohol or drugs shoring up my confidence?

"Jesus, Alex, what have you been eating? There's not much to work with."

"Sorry. We can order in. I just order in."

"No, you need something home-cooked. I'll make it work, but Jesus, seriously." He stuck his head around the corner and shook it at me, but his eyes were smiling. I smiled back.

I wasn't happy, that's for sure. If I wasn't happy doing it, why was I still doing it? What more would I lose? How strong would I let the addiction become before enough was enough? Would I be able to stop later if I didn't stop now?

"I don't hear cleaning," Steven called from the kitchen.

There was a lot of cleaning up to do, I knew, and not just the mess in the living room. I had to apologize to Brandon for having Allan over. I had to apologize to Dinah for my scene at her bachelorette party. I had to try to get my job back. I had to talk to Aaron. I had to talk to Jesse. It was a long list of amends to be made, and it weighed heavy on me, and made me want to do nothing more than scrape together one more line off that mirror and forget about it all.

I stood up and made a decision. This was not the person I wanted to be. I couldn't let Nathan have this kind of power over my life. I couldn't even blame it on Nathan. There had been drugs before him. There had definitely been drinking before him.

I remembered the first time I got drunk. It was the day of Taylor's funeral. Dinah stole some beer from her dad's fridge and we sat out behind her garage and slammed them back. I didn't want to talk, and she didn't force the issue. He was gone, and right then, it seemed like the bullies would win. The bigger kids who used to circle me on their bikes and call me faggot. The guys like Nathan, like Taylor's dad. They had killed him, as surely as if they had pulled the trigger themselves. Getting drunk seemed like the only way I could escape the thoughts that filled my head, that they would always win, that I should do it too, that I would never find anyone who I loved like I loved Taylor.

"What are you doing?" Steven came out of the kitchen to see me just standing there, gin bottle in one hand, mirror in the other.

"I'm throwing this all out," I said, and marched into the kitchen and put them in the garbage, then sealed up the garbage bag and walked down the hallway to the garbage chute and placed the bag at the top of the chute, and let go.

I turned around to go back to the apartment and Steven was watching me. He was smiling, and his smile wasn't sad or a half smile or a patronizing smile. It was filled with pride and love, and it made me smile back, even as a part of me wanted to dive down the chute after the bag.

Even though things were bad, they had gotten better. The bullies didn't always win. And I had found someone who I loved like I loved Taylor. He was standing there in front of me, and I would get him back for good.

Chapter 31

I woke up alone. That wasn't unusual. I rarely let the Grindr tricks stay the night. They would come, then cum, then go, and I would polish off the booze and the blow and eventually pass out. So waking up alone wasn't unusual at all.

Waking up without a hangover, that was unusual.

I picked up Griffin and we walked out in the living room, where Steven was sleeping on the couch. He looked so cute, even with his hair messed, and his mouth open, and his stuttered snoring. I chuckled under my breath, but it must have been loud enough for him to hear me. He stirred, stretched, yawned. "Is it morning already?"

"I'll make some coffee," I said, and left him to wake up in peace.

It was unusual that he had slept over, but that we hadn't slept together. The first day we met, we ended up spending a whole weekend together. But last night, we had eaten dinner, and then watched another movie, and hadn't really talked, and hadn't touched. And then he said we should get to bed, and I thought he meant together, but he'd simply walked me to my bedroom door, and kissed me on the cheek, and then went back to the couch. I had lain there for a while, wondering if I should invite him down, wondering if a cuddle would be that out of the question, feeling anything but horny. But then I had fallen asleep sober, for the second time in weeks.

"I don't have much in the way of breakfast stuff," I said.

"You don't have much in the way of anything stuff," he said. "Don't worry. We'll get some groceries after we're done with Nathan."

Done with Nathan. Three simple words. Three super-complicated words. What would the morning entail? Would he admit to sending me the picture? And who did he get to shove it in my mailbox? And why? Why me? There were thousands of gay people in the world!

Why was Nathan so fixated on me? Would Nathan ever be done with me, because until he was, we would never be done with Nathan.

Steven came up behind me, and wrapped his arms around me. "You doing okay?" I murmured affirmatively as he nuzzled my neck. "Good boy. We'll grab a bagel or something on the way to the jail," Steven said. "I'm going to shower."

I thought of joining him, but it was too soon. I just wanted to rush this awkward part along, to get back to the comfort and ease we used to have. Life needed a fast-forward for moments like this, to skip past the fixing-things part, the getting-done-with-Nathan part, the edginess I was feeling as I prepared to face the day, the week, the life sober and clean.

Steven showered, then I showered, and neither of us said much until we were in Steven's car and headed out of town. I turned to him and said, "Thanks for taking me."

He smiled. "Of course. I want this all to be behind us too."

"I know, but this time, you didn't have to. It wasn't involving you."

"Anything that involves you involves me," he said, and moved his hand from the gearshift to squeeze my knee. "Especially anything that involves this psychopath."

"I almost went to see him once before," I confessed.

"Oh?"

"It wasn't too long after he got sentenced. I was actually about halfway there before I turned around."

"Why?"

"Why did I turn around? I just couldn't face him."

"No, why were you going to go?"

"Actually, to thank him. I know it sounds ludicrous, but I just wanted to thank him for confessing, for pleading guilty, for saving us all the ordeal of a trial."

"Never thank him. He doesn't deserve gratitude for that."

"I know."

"When was this?"

"A couple of weeks after . . . That Friday Night. Maybe I was drunk or high when it occurred to me. It just seemed like the right thing to do."

"Never trust what your brain tells you to do when you're fucked up. Better yet, don't get fucked up anymore."

"I'm going to try not to."

"I'm glad to hear that." He drove in silence for a minute or so. "How often are you doing it?"

Steven hated drugs. Before me, he'd been very much in love with a guy who was very much in love with coke, and Steven had come home to find his place cleared out, everything sold to pay off his lover's skyrocketing drug debt. Everything he had worked hard for, gone. The guy, Pierre, never even had the guts to face Steven.

That was why he hated drugs. And me doing coke had almost killed our relationship before. Now though, everything was as over as it could be, and if things were going to rebuild, they had to do so on an honest foundation. I knew that.

Still, all I could say was, "Too much."

"You know how I feel."

"I know. I know Pierre screwed you over."

"Fuck Pierre. This is about you. I worry about you. I don't want to see you dead."

"I know." We drove in silence for a while, and then I said, "Every weekend. Friday and Saturday both. Sometimes, during the week. Sometimes, just to get going again in the morning. Sometimes, to keep going when I'm almost passing out from being so drunk."

"So, too much?" He smiled, shaking his head.

I chuckled. "Yah, too much." I paused. "I'm done."

"Easy to say that, Alex."

"I mean it."

"What about next time you're drunk?"

"Done with that, too. I have to be. They go together for me now."

"That's going to be hard. You've got a lot of work ahead of you."

"I know."

"I'll help you as much as I can, though."

"What can you do? I just have to not do it."

"I know. But, you know, I'm here to talk or whatever."

"I know." I reached over and squeezed his knee. He reached down and squeezed my hand.

"I've missed you, Alex."

"I've missed you, too."

We drove on, leaving the city behind. The freeway stretched out ahead of us, the sun now high overhead. It was a beautiful spring day. This was about how far I had gotten that other time, before I turned back, still twenty minutes to the jail where Nathan was confined.

What would it be like to see him for the first time since the court session where he pled guilty? What would it be like to stare through the Plexiglas window at him, to pick up the little phone and hear his voice? Would he own up right away, or would we have to drag the confession from him?

"What are you thinking about?" Steven asked.

"How much of this is his fault," I said. "Can he really be held responsible for what he does? I can't even imagine having to go through everything he did. To be raped over and over again by your own father and his friends? Can we blame him for hating us?"

"We didn't do that to him, Alex. Yes, we can blame him. That's not gay people doing that. It's child molesters, and yes, it's terrible, but you even thinking that what happened to him makes what he did to us even a little bit excusable, you can't. If you do, he wins."

It echoed my own thought from earlier, and I turned back to look out the window, the countryside speeding by. And soon, there in the distance, I saw it. The Tulgey Federal Correctional Institution: sprawling, brown and gray, and fenced. It was uninviting, yet not nearly as foreboding as it should have been.

That changed though as we parked. With each step, it felt heavier on my heart. Each step of the procedures brought us closer to Nathan. We registered. We were scanned at security. And then we were eventually brought into a room filled with tables. There was no Plexiglas barrier. He would be directly across from us, much like another prisoner already was, in his orange, visiting a crying woman.

We would be at the same table as him. Like we were friends or family. Not like we were the victims of his rage and hate. There was a guard at the one entrance, and two at the other. We were safe. Of that, I had no doubt, but we would be at the same table as him.

Steven nudged me, and pointed me toward the door. There he was.

Chapter 32

His blond hair was cropped off. He had packed on muscle since the last time I had seen him, but it was almost too much. He looked swollen underneath that hideous orange jumper. Is this what regular people thought, when they came to visit people in prison? That no one could look good in such a shade of orange? Or was it just me (*faggot faggot faggot*)?

When he saw us, there was a brief confusion on his face, one that morphed into a sneer, before fading into passiveness. Steven clenched my knee under the table, and I let out the breath that caught in my lungs when I saw Nathan. He sauntered across the room and sat down across from us, sitting on the chair backward, cocky as always.

"Well," he said. "When they said I had visitors, I sure didn't expect it to be the two of you."

"Who else, Nathan?" Steven said. "You made it pretty clear when you were holding me hostage, there's no one in your life."

Nathan's expression shifted. Gone was his arrogance; in its place was a sudden panicked confusion. I smiled at Steven. He had my back. And then I realized how hard this must be for him. Yes, Nathan had been trying to get to me, but Steven had been his pawn. Steven was the one he had kidnapped and tortured. Steven was the one who could have died.

Not everything was about me.

It was a simple realization yet a profound one, and it clicked inside me. Not just regarding Steven, but also with Nathan. Maybe confronting him head-on wasn't the way to get either cooperation or a confession. Maybe I needed to see what it was like for him, and reach him that way.

"Look, Nathan, we're not here to fight."

"Why are you here then?"

"How are you doing?" His shock at my simple question was matched by Steven's.

"How am I doing? Really? How the fuck do you think?"

"I really want to know."

"You don't fucking care."

"I do. I know that what you did, it wasn't all your fault. I know—"

"You don't know! Don't pretend you know! Don't pretend like we're friends."

"I'm not, and we're not . . . but we were, once."

"Until you touched me with your disgusting faggot hands."

"I didn't know what he'd done to you, Nathan. I didn't know what he'd let them do to you."

"Look, I don't want to talk about this." He stood up. "I get enough therapy from the prison shrink, okay?"

"Sit down, Nathan," Steven said. "Alex, just ask him."

"Ask me what?" Nathan sat back down.

"I'm sorry for touching you. I'm sorry for shooting you. But this needs to stop, Nathan. You can't keep harassing me, harassing us, like this."

"What the fuck are you talking about, Alex?"

"The picture. I don't know how you got it to me, I don't know who you got to deliver it, but who else could it be from, Nathan? Who else would do that?"

"What are you talking about? I don't know anything about any picture."

"Nathan, look." Steven stood up now. I could see the guard watching us. "No more fucking around. We don't even care. Just admit it, and stop it, and it's done. We won't press any charges, we will just forget it ever happened, but you have to promise it's over."

"Promise what's over? I really have no clue what you fags are going on about."

"The picture of Taylor."

His face scrunched up in disgust. "Your little faggoty-ass boyfriend from high school? Why would I send you a picture of him?"

"Just to fuck with me! I'm done being fucked with, Nathan."

"I thought that's what you like," he said with a sneer.

"Nathan, I swear to God . . ."

I was standing up now, and the guard came over. "Okay, guys, keep it calm, or this ends."

"We're done," Steven said. "He won't tell us anything. You can take him away."

"Wait, wait. We can still talk," Nathan said. The guard looked at Steven, and Steven looked at me, and I nodded, and the guard walked back to his spot at the door.

"Okay, talk," Steven said.

"What is this about a picture of Taylor?"

"Look, if you're just going to play games . . ."

"I'm not! I swear. I just . . . I didn't send you anything, Alex. It wasn't me."

"Then why do you want to know about it?"

"I don't, really . . . I just don't want to go back yet. You were right," he said to Steven. "There's no one else to visit me."

"Oh no, this is not a social call. We are not your friends. Not after what you did to me." Steven got up again.

"Steven, sit," I said. "Look, Nathan, I'm sorry you're here, and I'm sorry you're alone." My eyes watered. Was I really crying over this psychotic piece of shit? "But no one else would have sent me that. No one."

He reached across the table and grabbed me by the wrist. "It wasn't me."

"No touching!" the guard yelled from across the room, coming back over.

"It wasn't me," Nathan said again, letting go.

"Then there's no reason for us to be here," Steven said. "C'mon, Alex, let's just go."

I stood up and we started to walk toward the door.

"Wait!" Nathan said, and we turned back to him, standing there, the guard's hand wrapped around his arm.

"What, Nathan? What?"

"I'm sorry." He stared at the floor as he said it, and I couldn't believe I was hearing the words. "I . . . I know it wasn't you . . . wasn't your fault. You didn't do . . . didn't do those things to me." He looked at me, his eyes burning into mine, and images flashed through my brain: us fighting for the gun, us fighting in the classroom the day

Taylor died, him screaming at me to get away from him, us laughing and playing and running in the park. “I’m sorry, Alex.”

“Sorry is just a word,” Steven said, and he practically dragged me from the room. I didn’t look back. I didn’t want to see him like that, in orange and beaten down. I wanted to remember him the other way instead, when the days were golden and he was my best friend.

Chapter 33

We didn't say much on the way back to the car. There wasn't much to be said. We got in and drove away, and we had no answers. Did I believe Nathan? Yes. After everything, after kidnapping Steven, after torturing him and tormenting me, and after nearly killing us both, I still believed him. It was just a feeling, but it was a feeling I felt was right.

I looked over at Steven, and his brow was furrowed as he stared straight ahead. His knuckles were white on the steering wheel. "What's wrong?" I asked.

"Just seeing him. Hearing him lie and lie and lie. I am just so mad."

"You're allowed to be mad after what he did."

"What he's still doing. I can't believe he won't give up. What's he trying to accomplish?"

"I don't know . . ." I started to say, and then Steven went on.

"Like, a picture of Taylor! How would he think you wouldn't know it was him? What game is he playing?" He turned to look at me. "You don't know what?"

"I . . ."

"You believe him."

"I don't know. Maybe . . . he seemed sincere."

"You're being pretty fucking gullible, Alex. First, you believed that little twink, when he never did anything but lie to you. And now you're believing Nathan."

"Don't get mad at me," I said. "It's just a feeling."

"Well, your feeling is wrong. Who else, Alex? Who else?"

Who else indeed? Who was in my life now that knew me then? Aaron came along long after Taylor was gone. It was so long ago. It was just me and Taylor. And Dinah. Dinah had been there. Dinah was still here, I hoped. I needed to fix that. I needed to apologize.

"Maybe Dinah would have an idea. She was there when he died."

"Well, let's call her and see."

"I haven't talked to her since her party. We . . . had a scene."

"I know. But you still haven't fixed that? Alex, it's been days. You and Dinah never go this long without talking."

"I just haven't had the strength."

"What did she do? Just blame you for me leaving?"

"She called me a fag."

"She didn't!"

"She didn't mean it. I know she didn't mean it, but the shape I was in, it just hit me hard, and I lost it."

"Well, just call her. You know she must feel as badly as you do."

"I know. There's just been so much happening since."

"That's part of your problem, Alex. You need to start dealing with things, not just letting them pile up. You let them take control of your head until they're too big to face, and then you do stupid shit like get drunk or high."

"I know. I'll call her when we get home."

"You'll call her now."

"Steven . . ."

"Call her, Alex. Call her and tell her we are on our way there."

"What?"

"Some things are easier in person."

"But—"

"Do it, Alex."

I took out my phone and took a deep breath. He was right. He was always right. Infuriatingly and painfully right, but right. A text would be easier. A text would probably be all it would take.

"Call her. You're not texting."

"But—"

"Alex."

I sighed, but dialed. It rang once, twice, three times.

"I'm sorry," she said, in place of hello.

"I'm sorry," I said, in place of hello.

"We're good?"

"We're good."

"Good."

"Good."

"How are you?"

"Not good."

"What's up?"

"Can we come over?"

"Who's we?"

"Me and Steven."

"You and Steven?"

"Me and Steven."

"What's going on, Alex?"

"Some things are better said in person. We'll be there in about half an hour?"

"Should I be worried?"

"No. We just need to ask you something."

"Of course come over. I have something to tell you, too."

"See you soon then." I hung up. "There. Better?"

"Good boy, Alex," Steven said with a smile, and he squeezed my knee.

Chapter 34

Everyone I knew lived in the gayborhood. Most were in condos high in the sky, overlooking the city, far removed from the homeless and the traffic and the ugly streets. Not Steven. He had his cute little house on his quaint little street. And not Dinah. At first, she too had lived in a condo in the clouds, but she and Christopher had moved out to the suburbs, where all straight couples eventually ended up. In a cul-de-sac even! It was all very *Knots Landing.*

We pulled up outside, but as I opened the door, Steven grabbed my arm and pulled me back in.

"What . . ."

He kissed me briefly, too briefly. And then pulled away.

"Why?"

"It felt like the thing to do. You're doing good." He looked at me. "You are doing good, right?"

"You're here, I'm doing great." I smiled. He smiled. "Let's go talk to Dinah."

We walked up the sidewalk to their door, past the chain-link that served as a replacement for white-picket fencing, past the lawn gnomes sitting there in the dirt waiting for flowers. I loved her, but damn, the girl could be tacky. Lawn gnomes, Dinah? Really? We had barely rung the bell before she bounded out of the door into my arms. Lawn gnomes or no, I did love her.

"Come in, come in, come in," she said, "Christopher is at work but come in." She ushered us into the living room, which was simple but comfortable. "Can I get you guys something to drink?"

"Not gonna lie," Steven said, "I'd love a gin."

"Sure. You too, Alex?"

"No. Just a water for me."

Steven smiled at me as Dinah went to get the drinks. "You don't mind that I'm having a drink drink? Sorry, that was really insensitive of me. It's just, after seeing Nathan . . ."

"You don't have to apologize. I understand. This is my problem, not yours."

"I know, but—"

"You're just concerned. I get that, and love you for it. It's good though. I'm good."

Steven was looking at me, and then I realized what I had said. The *L* word. It had been a while since either of us had dropped that. Too long, but still so true.

Dinah came back in with the drinks and handed them out. "Not drinking, Alex?"

"No. It's time to stop."

"I'm glad to hear that," she said with a smile. "I'm stopping too."

"Oh why?" I asked, and then it dawned on me. That inevitably heterosexual ending. "You're pregnant?"

"Yes!" She practically squealed. "We just found out today! Oh Alex, I'm so happy."

I went over and hugged her, my best friend of so many years. "I'm so happy for you," I said, and I was. It filled me up with light and warmth inside. She was glowing. She was bringing a new life into the world. She would raise that baby to love everyone, just the way she did. And baby by baby, the world would become a better place.

"Okay, Alex, you can let go now," she said, squirming under the hug that had gotten far too intense. I smiled, she smiled, and then all three of us laughed.

"And of course, Alex, I want you to be godfather."

"Absolutely," I said, without hesitation. I was an only child. I would have no nephews or nieces. Steven, too, was an only child, so even if we worked things out, I wouldn't be an uncle ever that way either. Dinah's kid was my only chance to scratch that paternal itch (unless Steven and I adopted some distant day . . .). Either way, her kid, or our future kid, was simply one more reason that the booze-and-blow Alex had to go away.

"So, what's up with you?" She was beaming, and the way she asked, I knew she expected the news to be that we had worked things out and were getting back together. Could I disappoint her? Again? And what's more, could I bring something so dark into her world, when she was so filled with hope and light?

"You have to, Alex," Steven said, and I looked at him looking at me, and knew he knew exactly what I was thinking. He always did.

"Something happened," I said. "I got a picture of Taylor in the mail." She slumped back into her chair, and just as I feared, the light drained from her as I told her about the graffiti (*faggot faggot faggot*), the picture (*You killed me*), and about confronting Allan and Nathan. By the end, she was crying.

"Who would do that?" she said. "I don't understand . . ."

"Me either," I said. "But you're the only person I know who I knew when Taylor died. I can't come up with anyone other than Nathan. Can you?"

She sat there, her eyes closed, the odd tear trickling down her face. Steven, next to me on the couch, put his arm around my shoulders and I squeezed his thigh as a thank you.

"There's no one else I know of. You were his only friend, really."

"He liked you, too," I said.

"I know, but you were his friend. He was just so new still. Just there a year. No one really had the chance to get to know him. You know how it was in high school. It took forever for new kids to find a clique that would accept them. And Taylor didn't want a clique. He just wanted you."

Hearing her say it set my nose to tickling with tears. I pushed tears away with the heels of my hands. I could not cry. I would not cry.

"It's okay to cry," Steven said, and I looked at him, and his eyes were watery, too, and I cried.

"I had always known there was something different about you, Alex," Dinah said. "But it wasn't until Taylor came along that I figured out what it was. Seeing you together was . . . right. It was the part of you that was missing. I knew you were gay long before you told me, you know that. I think I even knew before you did. I saw it when you two looked at each other. Everyone saw it.

"That was part of the problem. Everyone saw it. I felt so terrible every time I would hear what they would say about you. But what could I do? And then something amazing happened. You didn't need my help. The stronger you made each other, the more you ignored what they said, and the more you ignored what they said, the less they said it. By the time he . . . by the end, I think it was only Nathan I ever heard say anything, and it was sad when he said it. Like a man who lost an argument, and everyone knew he had lost except him."

Hearing her talk took me back there, back to high school, back to him. The first time I saw him. The first time we kissed. The first time we fucked. The last time I saw him. The last time I said I loved him. How badly had his death fucked me up, that it still hurt so bad so many years later? I was thirty. I was all grown up. High school was a lifetime ago. Two lifetimes ago.

"It still hurts," I said aloud, barely realizing I was talking.

Steven held me tighter and Dinah started crying anew. She moved to the couch next to me, and hugged me. I shook. Now in my head, when I thought his name, instead of seeing the way his bangs flopped over his forehead, I just saw the picture (*You killed me*). Who sent it? Who?

And what would they do next?

Chapter 35

We stayed at Dinah's for an hour or so, shooting the shit about happier things, mostly her pregnancy and plans for when the baby came. Dreams of the future. The kind of talks Taylor and I used to have, lying on the roof, staring at the stars, ready for a time when there wouldn't be bullies, when we wouldn't have to hide who we were and how we felt about each other.

If only he had been strong enough to wait. If only he had been strong enough to survive.

When we left Dinah's, Steven stopped off at a grocery store and grabbed some supper. We didn't discuss him coming over. It was just understood. I didn't want to be alone. He didn't want to be alone. The pain and anger I had felt about what happened between him and Aaron, between us and Aaron, it seemed so stupid now. This was real, not some stupid threesome or some jealous delusion I had concocted in my head.

We didn't talk much. The day had left us both pretty drained emotionally, and while we made dinner, we fell into our old pattern, working around each other, in perfect sync. As we ate, we'd occasionally smile at each other. It was nice and simple, and a change from what had been the norm for too long. Right then, right there, there was no Nathan or Aaron or Allan or Taylor, no cocaine, no alcohol, no jealousy.

It was Alex and Steven.

It was as it should be.

"Let me clean up," Steven said, "you go lie down."

"No. I'll clean. You can go if you want."

"I don't want to."

"You can stay," I said, "of course, and I'll love the company. But I'm still going to clean."

"I won't argue," he said, and he brushed his hand across my back as he went into the living room.

What was happening? Was this the beginning of the beginning again? Could he really forgive me for what I had done and said during the crazy darkness of the past months? He was here, and that said a lot. I washed up the dishes, with hope bubbling up inside me. The thought that we could truly put the past in the past and get back to where we had been, before the Caterpillar, before Nathan . . .

When the dishes were done, Steven was half-dozing on the couch. He looked so peaceful. I stood there, again, looking down on him and smiling. I knelt beside the couch and shook him. "Hey, do you want to go to bed?"

He stirred. "No, just come lie down here on the couch with me. Let's watch a movie."

He was big spoon to my little spoon again, and oh! How good his arms felt around me. It wasn't long before our breathing synchronized, too, and my eyes were just getting too heavy to stay open when he pulled me in closer and nuzzled my neck, his breath warm and sweet. "God, I've missed this. I love you, Crazy."

"I love you, too," I said, my face flushed in bliss as I yawned and let myself sink into the safety of him, my Steven.

I was half-in, half-out of sleep, so at first, I wasn't sure if I was dreaming or not, but no, it was real. I could feel him getting hard behind me, and my body reacted in kind. His hips pumped into me, and his mouth, still at my neck, started to tongue my earlobe. As his hand slid down my chest to my suddenly throbbing erection, I let out a groan.

"Is this okay?" he asked, his fingers undoing my jeans.

To answer, I reached behind me, slid my hand down the back of his pants, and pulled him in closer. His ass still felt amazing, and yes, I wanted to fuck him again, but my need to feel him in me was far more urgent. Many men had touched me since we broke up. I had wanted none of them the way I wanted Steven. My want was sober and pure and literally leaking from me as I twisted around in his arms and found his mouth with mine.

The second our lips met, everything else was gone. We were feeding on each other, two starving men desperate to consume everything in front of them. Clothes peeled off and went flying across the room, and our bodies were soon naked together, like they were meant to be. I pushed him down on the couch and started sucking him. He was thrusting his hips and I could tell by the way he was moaning that this could be a quick cum. That was one of the things I loved about him. He could shoot in minutes or he could last for what seemed like hours.

Right now though, I wanted it hard and fast, and I wanted him in me. I climbed up, straddled him, and reached over him to where I kept lube and condoms in the end table. My phone rang, somewhere. I barely heard it. I rolled a condom down his shaft, smeared it in lube, and guided it to my waiting, hungry hole.

I slid down on it. It stabbed me and my moan was loud and long. Steven was thrusting below me, eager to start pumping, but I was in control. I leaned down and kissed him, and he was all the way in. My phone rang again, but I was flexing my ass, squeezing, teasing, pleasing his cock, and I started to ride him.

"I won't last long," he said. "Fuck, how I've missed you, missed being inside you, missed you kissing me."

"Shhh," I said. "Don't talk, and don't worry. Just enjoy."

He started stroking my dick as I rode him, his hand slick with lube. I almost shot right then, and both our bodies quivered together. His hand milked me as my ass milked him, and then suddenly, he tensed underneath me, and I could feel him fill the condom inside me. His hand froze on my dick as he shot, and I looked down to see me spray all over his face and chest.

Panting, laughing, I lay down on him, my load sticky between us. His dick plopped out of my ass, and I wanted him back in.

My phone rang again.

"Jesus Christ!" I said.

"You better get that. I'll go shower."

I looked for my phone as I watched him walk down the hall to the bathroom, cum-covered and gorgeous. I found it where it had fallen and answered it. "Hello?" I said, still out of breath.

"Hello."

"Who is this?"

"Who is this?"

"Look, you called me. Who's this?"

"It's Taylor."

Chapter 36

The fuck?

"That's not funny," I said.

"It's not a joke. It's Taylor."

"Taylor's dead."

"Taylor's dead," he repeated.

"Stop it!"

Steven came running back down the hall. "What is it?"

Shaking, I handed him the phone. "Who is this?" he yelled. I couldn't hear his answer. "Look, stop this now. Do not call here again."

He threw the phone down and threw his arms around me. "Who was it? What did they say?"

"They said . . . he said . . . he said he was Taylor."

"That's ridiculous, Alex. It's just a prank. It's just a horrible, cruel prank. Taylor's dead."

I was sobbing, rocking back and forth in his arms. Oh, I wanted a drink! Or drugs! Or anything that could make it so I didn't have to think or feel. Why this? Why me? Why Taylor? Who was doing it?

My phone rang again. We didn't answer. It rang and it rang, stopped ringing, and then rang and rang again.

"Leave it," Steven said. "Don't engage him. That's what he wants. Whoever it is, whatever game he is playing, that's what he wants."

"But . . ."

"Alex, look at me, listen to me. You know it wasn't Taylor. It's a fucked up thing to do, but it wasn't him."

And it wasn't. I knew that. Taylor was dead. I had been to his funeral. No, we hadn't seen the body. It had been a closed casket, of course. He'd shot himself in the head.

But what if . . . ? It came to me, a vision of what might have been, and even though I knew it was the result of growing up on soap operas and melodrama, what if he hadn't killed himself? What if it had all been a ploy? And the funeral was faked? And he was still alive, after all these years?

It was fantastical, and ridiculous, and completely impossible. Things like that didn't happen. I knew that. Logically, I knew that. But part of me wanted it to be true.

My phone chimed, the voice mail indicator.

"Leave it," Steven said.

"No, I need to hear it." I put it on speakerphone and gripped Steven's hand as I pressed play.

"AAAAAAAAAAAAAAAAALEX. It's Taaaaaaaaaaaaaylor. Did you miss me? I missed you. I haven't seen you since you kiiiiiiiiiiiiiiiilled me. Remember that, Alex? When you made me gay and I had to go away? You might as well have shot me yourself."

Steven got up and turned the phone off. "This is it," he said. "Tomorrow, we are changing your number. You can come stay with me for a while. We will figure out who is doing this, Alex. We will get through this. Together." He looked me in the face. "And we will get through this sober. You don't need anything else."

"I don't. You're right." I was vibrating, and realized that my cry had been a pretty messy, snotty one. Hardly the kind of face I wanted to show my ex-but-maybe-not-for-long boyfriend. I covered my face. "Oh God, don't look at me." It was half nervous laugh, half panicked cry.

"Don't be silly. I don't care that you're a mess. I would be too. Hell, I was too. You saw what I was like when I was gone. When you found me." He cradled my face in his hands. "And you did find me," he said. "Nothing else matters, but that you saved me. And now, I am going to save you."

He took me by the hand and led me down the hall. We showered, showered off the sex, showered off the tears. I never let go of him. Constantly, I touched him. His shoulder. His arm. His hand. I was always holding on to him.

After the shower, he tucked me into bed, and without me asking, he crawled in next to me. "I won't sleep," I said.

"I know. Just try."

He lay there next to me as I curled up fetally, clinging on to him, and not even caring if it made me seem pathetic. He was right. He was all I needed. His hand tracing patterns of nothing on my back drove away more demons than the Caterpillar's finest ever had. I could hear his heart beat and lost myself in that sound. His chest rose, his chest fell. His chest rose, his chest fell. His chest rose . . .

I woke up in a stereotype. The mist curled around the tombstones and the trees were bare. The sky above me was blue.

"Alex."

I turned around and there he was. I knew he would be here, knew he was why I was here. His bang was flopping across his face, and I reached out to brush it away. "Hi, Taylor."

"Two hearts, one heart."

I froze. It was what we always said, and I hadn't expected to hear it. I had forgotten it. It was one of the last things I said to him. The last night I saw him. The night he took his father's gun and shot himself. I had always wondered. Was he thinking of those words when he pulled the trigger?

"I still miss you," I said. "Every day, part of me still misses you."

"I had to go," he said. "I had to."

"Why, Taylor? Why?"

"They always win, Alex. The bullies always win. Hate always wins. We can't fight it. It won't change."

"It has though, Taylor. It's gotten better."

"Has it? Have things gotten better for you? Were things better when Nathan took your boyfriend hostage? Were things better when you were getting high and getting fucked by anyone that came along? That wasn't the future we planned for us. That wasn't two hearts, one heart. Has it gotten better?"

"Yes, it has."

He smiled sadly and shook his head. "I don't believe you. If it's better, then what's this?"

He handed me a piece of paper and I knew what it was before I even unfolded it. You killed me.

"I didn't kill you."

"You made me know I was different. If I hadn't figured that out, I wouldn't have had to go."

"I didn't do it."

"You did. You gave me hope. You gave me love. But they wouldn't let me have it. Not that kind of hope. Not our kind of love." He looked

at me. "Faggot faggot faggot!" he yelled out suddenly, stepping toward me. His hands were on my shoulders. "That's what he said as he beat me. That night my mom found us. 'Faggot faggot faggot.' As he hit me over and over and over and over and over. . . ."

"Stop it!"

" 'Faggot faggot faggot! No son of mine! No son of mine! I'd rather you be dead than a fucking fruity faggot queer! No son of mine! Faggot faggot faggot.' "

"Stop, please, Taylor, stop."

"That's what I said. 'Stop, Daddy, stop.' He didn't stop. They wouldn't stop. They wouldn't ever stop, Alex. I had to go. And that's how you killed me. You gave me something better, but they would keep taking it away."

The cemetery was gone, and we were at his house now. The last place I saw him alive. The place where he died. The tree outside his bedroom window was bare. The streets were dark, the house was dark. And the light was on in the garage. Taylor walked toward it. I didn't want to follow him. I knew what would happen.

"Stop."

"It doesn't stop."

"Please."

"Stop, Daddy, stop."

"Taylor . . ."

"No son of mine."

"Two hearts, one heart . . ."

He was at the garage door. It was rising. He looked back at me. "Faggot faggot faggot." The door opened and bang!

I woke up, panting. Steven woke up beside me. "Are you okay? Bad dream? What's wrong?"

"We need to go somewhere tomorrow."

"Sure," he said. "Anywhere. Where do you wanna go?"

"Taylor's house."

Chapter 37

I woke up to find Steven had already made breakfast. That was just like him. Our first weekend together, he'd taken me for brunch both days, at the Duchess with all his friends. But the second weekend, when we both knew this was more than a one-weekend stand, I woke up to breakfast in bed, served on a tray with a flower from his garden in a vase. It was corny as hell, and I loved him for it.

This wasn't breakfast in bed, but it was omelettes and coffee and a good morning kiss, and it was practically perfect.

Practically, because there were three people in that room. Me and Steven and the ghost of Taylor.

"Now," Steven said, "tell me, why do you want to go to Taylor's old house?"

"Not just his house. I want to see my house, where we first kissed. I want to go by our school. I want to visit his grave. I need to figure out who is trying to resurrect him, and the only way I can think of doing it is to go home."

"Remember that day we talked about going back there? You were going to show me all the places you grew up. This wasn't quite how I pictured it happening."

I smiled back at him. "No, me neither. But lots of things didn't happen quite the way I pictured."

"That's true. Are we going to see your parents while we're there?"

My parents. That hadn't even occurred to me. It did seem ridiculous to drive the two hours to get there and not see them. When was the last time I'd seen them? They'd come to visit right after what happened with Nathan. How could they not have? Of course it had made news. That was the first time they'd come to see me, the first time they met Steven. All under less than ideal circumstances.

It wasn't that we weren't close. We just all had our own lives. When Aaron and I were together, we'd gone there for dinner once a month. Aaron was the first boyfriend they met. None of the guys from college lasted long enough to be worth the introduction, and yes, they knew Taylor of course, but didn't know he was a boyfriend until after he was gone.

Coming out had been a grief-stricken accident. I hadn't planned on doing it until after high school, until I moved out. But in the wake of Taylor's suicide, everything leaked out from me. Maybe that helped. The pain was exploding from me; how could they react badly? Or maybe, they just genuinely didn't care. Maybe I was one of the lucky kids. Not like Taylor.

"Yes, we'll see them. I don't want to stay there though."

"Oh, you can suck it up. It's just one night."

"Thank you for doing this with me, Steven. I really appreciate it. I really appreciate you."

"I wouldn't let you go through this by yourself. Are you almost done? We should go."

"Yeah, let's do this." I smiled at him, and started clearing the table. "Let me just wash these before we go."

"You go shower, I'll clean up. I don't mind."

"Why are you being so amazing?"

"Because you deserve amazing, Alex. And apparently, it's my job to remind you of that."

It was white fire rushing through me, but this time, it was his words and not cocaine. I felt my eyes tear up. "Thank you." I hugged him, and he hugged me back, and the hug got harder and harder and harder, and then he finally pulled away with a playful ass squeeze and said, "Quick, shower."

I laughed and obeyed. While I showered, I thought how it might actually be really nice, getting out of the city with Steven. We had only done it a couple times, last summer, short little day trips. We had never really had the chance. It would be open road, windows down, music up, laughing and talking and probably singing along to whatever was playing on the stereo. It would be clearing away the rubble of the past six months and getting back to where we had been before Nathan.

I still had the ring.

Maybe, one day, he would be wearing it again. For real. For good.

But in the meantime, a road trip back home, away from the gayborhood with its taint of drugs and sex and psychos, was just what we needed.

I got out of the shower, and Steven called to me, "Don't forget to change your number."

It was a cloud passing over the sun. Yes, there was a reason for this road trip, and that reason had my number. Luckily, it was easy enough to change it online now, and what's more, it's not as if I needed to update a bunch of people with the new digits. My contact list was small these days.

I turned my phone on, and took a deep breath when the voice mail indicator was there. How many more times had he called last night after Steven turned it off? I sat there on my bed, staring at it. Did I even want to hear it? Want to? No. Had to? Yes.

"Remember the time you killed me, Alex? That was fun. Did you feel better when my head was blown off? Did it make you feel happy and GAY? Stupid little faggot."

"Just delete it," Steven said, appearing in the doorway. "Delete it, change your number, and c'mon. Let's do this thing."

I cleared the voice mail, not even listening to the other four. I pulled out my laptop, logged into my cellular account, and surfed through the site to find where I could change my number myself. And just like that, it was done. All the while, Steven stood behind me, rubbing my shoulders. He leaned down and kissed me, when it was done.

"Let's go," he said. "I'll drive."

I packed up some toiletries and a change of clothes. We stopped by Steven's so he could do the same. Seeing his house brought that fist back around my heart. I hadn't seen it since That Friday Night. In none of my drunken and high self-destructive states had I gone there. Texted from home, sure. Left slurred voice mails of adoration and hatred, sure. But not gone back to the scene of That Friday Night.

Maybe that was a step I needed to take too. I needed to de-capitalize that in my head. It was just a Friday. It was just a night. It just happened. It was in the past now. We were moving on. It had been a mistake, but one we had made together. If Steven could forgive me, I could forgive him. And really, maybe, just maybe, he hadn't done much of anything wrong. It was a risk you ran when you started playing with three-ways. Things got complicated.

It was time to simplify things.

Soon, we were across the bridge, leaving the gayboyhood behind, driving through suburbia. I called my parents, to let them know my new number and to let them know they could expect us. They sounded excited. How long had it been since I had talked to them? They didn't know there'd even been a breakup, and they sure didn't know about the drugs.

Coming out as gay had been hard enough. Coming out as a drug-addicted, whoring fuckup was just not necessary.

"You should text everyone else. Let them know the number change."

"Most of them don't want to talk to me."

"New number for a new Alex," Steven said, with his charming smile. I reached across the car and squeezed his thigh. And then playfully squeezed his crotch. He laughed and slapped my hand away. "I'm driving. Stop it, Crazy!"

I laughed and typed out, **This is a new Alex, and this is his new number. New starts.** I sent it to Dinah, to the twins (not expecting a reply from Jesse), to Brandon (not expecting a nice reply at all). I sent it to Walter and Mr. C. That was pretty much everyone, except for Aaron. Was he the next thing to try to fix? Could there really be a healthy, uncomplicated, nonsexual, non-emotionally-tangled place for him in my life?

"What are you thinking about?" Steven asked. We were nearing the city outskirts, and I was staring out the window. How could I answer his question honestly? Whatever doubt I had about what had or had not happened between him and Aaron, he had to have as many doubts, and more, about what had happened between Aaron and me.

"Who to send the new number to." That was true, and safe.

"The boys. Dinah," he said, and then looked at me. "Aaron."

How did he do that? Was my face really that much of a giveaway? How did he always know what was going on inside my head?

"You're overthinking. It's just a number."

"I haven't talked to him since . . . since, well, you know since when. Not talked to. Just crazy drunk shit."

"I know. We all got the texts and messages. I always knew you were a little crazy, right from the day you backed into my car to meet me. But damn, some of those voice mails were pretty out there. He understands though."

Jealousy tugged at me. "Oh, does he?"

"Alex," he said warningly, "don't do that. We talked, yes. We were worried about you. He was a big part of your past. Text him. He might not reply. But at least you've kept the door open."

I thought about it, and nodded. **Aaron. It's Alex. New number. And sober for a change. Don't need to reply. Just wanted you to have it.**

My finger hesitated a bit before hitting SEND, but hit SEND I did.

I turned my phone off and put it down. I looked at the window. We were on the highway now, fields all around us. Behind us, I could see the towers of downtown fading into the distance. Behind us was the Caterpillar, the Hole and Boyz and Wonderland. Behind us was Allan and Aaron and Nathan. That was all behind us.

Ahead of us was the open road. And home.

Chapter 38

I had fallen in love with the city the first time I had gone there. Well, the first time as a grown-up anyway. We'd gone when I was a kid. Even though there were plenty of malls back home, millions more people meant a million more stores, and once a year, Mom and I would drive the two and a half hours to go shopping. I hated it. By the time I was brave enough to tell her I hated it, I was old enough to stay home alone while Dad was at work, and so ended my adventures in the city.

Until college. His name was Jeffrey and I had met him at Trix. We had a great night of amazing sex, and the next morning, he asked if I wanted to ditch Smalltown and head into the Real City. There was a club there, he said, called Twist, and it would blow me away. Trix was great, he said, for a small town. It was part dance club, part pool hall, part restaurant, part boring-as-fuck. Every gay boy, he said, needed to go to Twist.

And so we went. The drive there was filled with loud music and meaningless conversation. We didn't really have much in common, it seemed. He worked retail, and seemed quite content to do that for the rest of his life. I wanted more than that out of life. He had opinions on everything and everyone, most of which were negative, and none of which I cared about. But I was excited to see this amazing club.

When I first saw the skyline, my heart skipped a beat. I knew right then that I would live there someday, in the towers in the sky. The sun was going down, and the sky was red, and the buildings were dark against it. But as we got farther into it, they were anything but dark. Everything was lit up, glowing golden in the new-fallen night.

Everything was alive. The streets were still filled with people. I strained my neck trying to take it all in.

We pulled up outside of Twist, with its velvet ropes and its lineup of people already waiting. Jeffrey bolted out of the car and ran to some people he knew in line. I walked quietly along behind him, and he eventually saw me and introduced me to the people we were now best friends with: a Derek, a Dustin, a Troy. They talked, they gossiped, they bitched. I took it all in.

Inside, it was pretty opulent, that's for sure. It was disco balls back home, and a chandelier here. It was bar lines back home, and roped-off VIP seating for bottle service from shirtless guys in tight black pants here. It was cute guys back home, and walking models here. They gawked, they gossiped, they bitched. I took it all in.

We didn't say much on the way home. Well, I didn't say much. Jeffrey talked nonstop about the numbers he got, the numbers he didn't get, gossip about people I didn't know and didn't care to know. I had been given a glimpse into a bigger, better, more brilliant world, and I was savoring every moment of it.

We fucked again that night, Jeffrey and I. Facedown in the pillow, he didn't talk, and so I topped with pleasure. The next morning, after he left, I got a text saying he didn't think things were going to work out. I was too quiet, too shy for him. He wanted someone a bit more outgoing.

I didn't mind in the slightest. A few weeks later, I met a boy named Aaron, and he asked me out on a date. And as the next six years began, I never forgot the way I felt when I first saw what the real city had to offer me as an adult gay man.

When I moved there finally, after Aaron and I were done, Twist was long since closed, and Jeffrey and his boys, who knew where they had gone. I wouldn't recognize one of them now if he was sitting on my face. I was sad to find that the club I had longed for was gone, but I was in the city, and that was magic enough for me. Until I met Steven, and he took me to a place called Wonderland.

But now, coming after all the shit that was Nathan and Allan and the drugs and the booze and the drama and the three-ways and the voice mails and pictures in the mail, coming after all the bullshit, the city seemed pretty tainted, and it was good to be headed home.

The miles passed by us, mostly in silence. Occasionally, one of us would say something inane. Occasionally, one of us would catch the other looking at him, and smile as he blushed and turned away. Something was turning around for us. I could feel it. Out here on the open road, in the open air, away from that magical city.

Did every gay man go all *Wizard of Oz* when he got closer to the place he called home? Maybe, maybe not. I sure did though, and there truly was no place like it.

Chapter 39

TAYLOR HOWARD - 1984–2001.

That's all it said.

No "Beloved Son." Not even a simple "Rest in Peace."

Why I insisted we start at the cemetery was beyond me. Maybe just because that's where my dream had been. Maybe because I wanted to make sure there was really a grave. I had never seen it before. All the class was at his funeral (his mom was weeping and wailing, his dad was nowhere to be seen). I had hid at the back not wanting to be noticed, just wanting to curl up and die myself.

I had wanted to go to the cemetery after the service in the church but that was when Dinah proposed getting drunk, and that sounded like a much better idea. Later, I had always had a reason not to go, and still later, it didn't seem important, and still later, it seemed important but I had now delayed going for so long that it was built up into this huge thing in my head and I knew it would take something drastic for me to ever set foot anywhere near Taylor's grave.

And here I was.

Here we were.

Steven was holding my hand, his other arm around my shoulders as I looked down on the grave that marked the final resting place of my first love. Just a name and two years. Is that all that was left? A warm memory in my heart, a pile of bones under the ground, and some words chiseled cheaply into stone?

"How are you doing?" Steven's words were barely audible. My head felt stuffed. Too many thoughts, too many emotions. It was too bright outside to be standing here, looking down at his grave. There were lots of things I wanted to say, but I couldn't find the words. "Do you want some alone time?"

Again, with his mind-reading! I bit my lip and nodded, and Steven squeezed my hand and walked back to the car. The grave next to Taylor's had been freshly visited. There were flowers on it. Taylor's was bare. Maybe we should have stopped. Maybe I should have brought something. It was so bare. Such an empty tombstone. Such a mowed grave. That was a morbid thought. Someone mowed this. What kind of job was that, pushing a lawnmower around a cemetery? Or was it a riding mower? And if it was, did he have to be a good driver? I laughed out loud, seeing the picture of a drunk groundskeeper bouncing off tombstones.

"Jesus, Alex. That's not cool," I said aloud. My voice sounded weird in the silence. "Jesus, Taylor," I went on. "I'm sorry. I don't know what I'm saying. I don't know what I'm thinking. I don't even know what I'm doing here!"

I started to turn away, to walk back to Steven and his white Rabbit and drive off. There was no point being here. There were no answers.

But instead, I sat down, cross-legged on the grass, facing the tombstone, and started to talk. "That's Steven that was here with me. God, I love him. He's amazing, Taylor. He's the kind of guy I always knew I would end up with. He completes me. He knows what I am thinking even before I do. Kinda like you did. Remember how we would always finish each other's sentences? Right from day one. You and I were such a perfect pair. I am so glad we had the time we had together.

"Someone's using you to fuck with me, hey? At first, I thought it was Nathan. You remember Nathan. The hot ass asshole, you used to call him. He's certifiably insane. He's in jail though, and we went to see him, and he said he didn't send me that picture. And I believe him. Did you? Was it your ghost? Are you angry at me for not saving you? Are you angry at me for loving you? I wish we had locked the door that night. We should have stayed safe in the closet until high school was done. We could have gone off to college together like we planned. We could have had the life we dreamed of.

"If that had happened, if you hadn't done what you did, I never would have met my Steven. So I don't know if that's good or not. I love him, and he loves me. But you were my first love, and we were so perfectly happy when it was just you and me against the world, and no one else was around. Just Dinah. She's pregnant. I know, right? Pregnant. It's been so long since you've been gone, Taylor. Sometimes, I wonder if the face I see is what you really looked like. If I close my eyes, I can still taste your lips on mine that first night we kissed. After we stopped giggling. That was the most perfect moment of my life. Kissing you. That first time. It was when I knew who I was and who I wanted to be. It was when I knew that what those bullies had always known, they were right. Well, they weren't right. They knew it about me before I knew it about me, but they were wrong. It wasn't bad. It was right. You were right. We were right together."

I had been pulling blades of grass out as I talked and ripping them apart with my hands, and now the tears were starting to come and I was grasping that well-mown lawn and squeezing my fingers into the dirt. "Fuck, Taylor! I don't want to be here. I don't want to be sitting here crying like a . . . like a little faggot over this. I'm over thirty for fuck sake. This was all behind me. You were all behind me, Taylor. Why does it all of a sudden feel like I'm seventeen again, and I just lost you, and nothing will ever be right the way we were right?

"And that's total bullshit. See the guy in that car over there? He's right. He feels right when I'm with him, and when I'm not with him, part of me is missing. The best part of me is missing. The things I have done to that man, and he's still there. Still putting his life on hold so I can come cry at a fucking cemetery over some kid I loved half a lifetime ago. It's ridiculous! Oh my God, what am I even doing here? How is this my life? I'm talking to a fucking tombstone like it's my priest and counselor and lover all in one.

"Somewhere, someone wants me to do just what I'm doing. They want me to freak out and feel pain. They won't win, Taylor. I won't let them win. It's the same them that made you put that gun to your head and pull that trigger all those years ago. It's the them that took you from me. They're the fucking faggots, Taylor, not you and me. They're wrong. And every day, more and more people see that. The world is changing, Taylor, and oh I wish you had stayed long enough to see that. They lost, Taylor. I lost you, but they lost the war."

I stood up. TAYLOR HOWARD - 1984–2001. That wasn't all that he had left behind. Those were just words on a piece of rock. He had left behind something in me, and whatever that was, it was, for the first time, making me stronger than ever.

"C'mon, Crazy, bring it. Bring me what you got. I'm ready." I placed my hand on Taylor's tombstone. It was rough and real, but it was just a rock. "Good-bye, Taylor. I didn't kill you. You didn't even really kill you. They did. They've killed kids all over the country, with their hate and their fear and their ignorance, their arrogance. But they're going to die off, and sooner than later, no kid will die just because they dared to love.

"Two hearts, one heart, Taylor. I love you."

I walked away, to where Steven was waiting in his car. I opened the door and sat down and leaned across and kissed him hard and long.

"What was that for?" he asked, when I finally pulled away.

"Because you are everything I have ever needed or wanted, and my life is better with you in it, and no matter what has happened or will happen, nothing will ever change that I love you today and always," I said, the words stumbling out of my mouth. "And I just wanted you to know that."

His face flushed, and he stuttered trying to reply. "I . . . I . . ."

I put my finger over his lips. "You don't need to say anything. You just had to hear it."

"Thank you," he said, starting the car. "I love you, too." He looked at me, and his face was still red. "Where to?"

"Just drive. Let's just be anywhere but here."

Chapter 40

We drove around my hometown and I pointed out pieces of my past as we passed them. The elementary school I went to. The park I used to play in. The house where I grew up. There were shades attached to all those places. Nathan once lived across the street from that house. Taylor and I kissed in that park, more than once. Nathan and I had been best friends in those early years.

But showing them to Steven, seeing them through his eyes, I only saw them as places that made me into who I was, and right then, I was feeling pretty good about who that person was. Yes, I was unemployed, but yes, I could fix that. Yes, I maybe had a substance problem, but no, I wasn't craving anything, and hadn't even thought about it for a day.

We drove by the high school. That was a bit harder. There, in those walls, so much had happened. But it was a lifetime ago, and none of it mattered now.

And then we drove by Taylor's old house. The tree was gone, chopped down. The lawn was unruly. It looked deserted. I got Steven to stop there, and I sat in the car, holding his hand, and looking at the place where Taylor had lived and died. The garage was hard to ignore. That was where he had hidden, with his father's gun.

"It's okay," Steven said. "It's in the past. There was nothing you could have done."

"I know," I said, looking out at that house, that garage, that bedroom window. It was dark and deserted and there was nothing left of Taylor there. It was words on a rock. That's all it was.

"Let's go see my parents," I said. "I think I've seen everything I needed to see."

"Actually, Alex, I made us dinner plans. I told them we'd be there after."

"Oh? Where at?"

"I googled a place while you were at the gravesite. Had to find somewhere in this town that makes pumpkin ravioli." He smiled at me, and suddenly, I began flipping through a calendar in my head. Had it really been . . . Was today really . . . "One year ago today is when we met."

A year. Already a year. Only a year. And he remembered. He must have known it was coming. I would have. I should have. Here he was, on this visit with the ghosts of Alex past, and all the while, he was just waiting for me to remember that a year ago, I stalked his sexy-ass home from the grocery store and backed into his VW Rabbit and started off our summer together.

"I'm sorry, I didn't even clue in."

"You would have, if you hadn't had so much going on. Besides, it doesn't mean anything other than I'm glad I'm here, with you, today." He leaned over and kissed me. It was one of those kisses that start soft and just when you sigh and it starts to get deeper, it's over. "Let's go eat, Crazy."

The wine we had had a year ago was replaced with water, but it was like that again. The romantic atmosphere. Eating food off each other's plates. Maybe the pumpkin ravioli wasn't as good as back home, but it was still pretty good, because I was with Steven, and Steven was with me, and it was just the two of us. How it was supposed to be.

But if things were going to be fixed, he had to know something.

"I have a problem," I said.

"With your ravioli?" He smiled.

"No," I said, trying not to laugh. "No. With drugs and alcohol."

He looked at me. "I know."

"No, you don't know."

"You've told me, and you're going to try to stop." He paused. "No. You're going to stop."

"It's more than that. I needed them, Steven. Like, needed." I reached across the table and took his hand. "It's been a while. I thought it was just fun. And I know I told you before it was fun that was behind me. But . . ." I was staring at the wall behind him. I couldn't look him in the eye. "It's been with me for so long. I panicked," I said. "When

I was going to propose. I was so stupid, Steven. I am so sorry." I couldn't help but cry now. "Everything since has just been such a mess, and I've just been so lost. But I see it now. I see that all the booze and coke just took me further away from myself. From who I wanted to be. From who I wanted to be for you. For us."

"Alex . . ."

"No, I know what you're going to say. It has to be for me. Quitting. I can't stop for you, or for us. I have to do it for me. That's what I'm saying. I want to. Quit. For me, I mean. I don't want to be that person anymore."

Steven was crying too. And I knew I had made him cry for so many things over these past few months. This time, there was pride in his eyes. Pride, and love.

"Thank you, Steven."

"For what?"

"For coming to rescue me."

"You're the one who came to rescue me," he said.

"I just found you," I said. "You're saving me from myself, and that's amazing. I love you."

I lifted his hand to my mouth and kissed his fingers. He squeezed my hand tight and I let it drop. We finished dinner, and the sun was already starting to go down. It was warm out though, and we went for a walk around the park. I kissed Steven where a lifetime ago I had kissed Taylor. There were other people in the park. I felt them watching us. One couple, walking arm in arm, smiled at us as we held hands walking along the lake. Things were different now than they had been. I wasn't scared. I was with Steven, and things were right.

"We should get to my parents," I said. "They're going to be going to bed soon, and I know they'll want to visit." We headed back to the car, kissing once more in the twilight. "Let's not tell them anything though. I don't want them to worry."

"Of course not. It's your call."

"They're probably going to expect us to sleep together."

"That won't be a problem for me." He smiled. I loved his smile. I loved him.

"Or for me. I just didn't want to assume. I don't know . . . I'm not sure where we are."

"We're right here," he said, with a wave of his hand.

"I meant with us."

"I know what you meant. We're where we are, Alex. There's so much going on. We can't put any more pressure on. We're just . . . where we are."

"I love you."

"Love you, too. Let's go."

To get from the park where we had walked to where my parents now lived took us back down some of the same streets. Steven followed my directions as I stared out the window at the places I knew so well, my face against the cold glass. We were driving down the street of Taylor's house again when I saw it. A light on. In what used to be Taylor's bedroom.

"Stop please."

"Who knows who lives there now?" Steven said. "Are you sure?"

"Please. Just for a second."

He pulled up out front of Taylor's house again. I got out of the car. "What are you doing?" Steven asked.

"Just a second," I said.

I walked up to the house, my steps heavy. Was I going to knock on the door? It was just the one light on. It had been years, Steven was right. Who knew who lived here now? Even if it was still Taylor's family, what would I say? Would they want to see me? Of course not. I was outside of the window though, and I had to look in.

I stood under the tree, staring up at Taylor's bedroom window. I jumped up, grabbed a branch, and pulled myself into the tree. There was no curtain, and the light was on, and there was no one there. But I knew the room. I knew the desk. I knew the bed. Nothing had changed. It was Taylor's room, frozen in time. Nothing had changed in thirteen years. The jacket on the chair at the desk was Taylor's jacket.

"Who are you?" I spun around at the sound of a woman's voice. "What are you doing here?"

"Sorry, I . . ." I saw her, standing there. I knew this woman. "Mrs. Howard?"

"Sorry, do I know you?"

"Yes. It's Alex Lewison. I was friends with your son."

"Alex? Is that really you?" Her hands, which had been on her hips, dropped to her sides. "But why . . ."

"I'm sorry, I don't know what I was thinking. I didn't mean to disturb you."

"Well, you did. Traipsing about in the middle of the night. What are you doing here?"

"I don't know."

"Is everything okay?" It was Steven, coming up the driveway, past the garage.

"Yes. Steven, this is Taylor's mom. Mrs. Howard . . ."

"Don't say that name!" Her voice was like a whip. Her face grew stony, and then softened. "Sorry, please, just don't say his name. I try not to ever say it."

"We're sorry to disturb you. We'll just go."

I started to walk away. I met Steven and we headed back to the car.

"Alex . . ." she said softly behind me. "I never thought you'd come here . . ."

"Again, I am sorry. I was in town, and I just . . ." I didn't know what to tell this woman.

"I know what you just. I just the same. You've come all this way. You might as well come in now. We can talk for a bit. Just please, don't say his name."

I looked at Steven, who half-nodded, half-shrugged. I looked back at Mrs. Howard, and half-smiled. "Okay."

Chapter 41

It was eerie, stepping foot in that house. I was stepping back in time. Everything was still the way it had been. The furniture was the same, in the same spots. It was quiet, too quiet. Steven was right at my side, and Mrs. Howard was just a few steps in front of us. The house was the same, but she wasn't. If the house hadn't aged a day, she had aged two for every one that had passed.

"Please, have a seat," she said.

We sat on the couch, and she sat in a chair across from us. She stared at us, through us. Minutes passed.

"It's a lovely home you have here," Steven said, awkwardly attempting to break the silence.

"Why, thank you," she said, looking around as if she were seeing it for the first time. "It's not much, but we call it home."

"Is your husband coming home soon?"

"What? Oh, no. He isn't here anymore. He's . . ." She looked around, and then looked at us. "Alex. You're all grown up. I wonder . . ."

"Wonder what?" I asked, dreading the answer.

"Wonder what he would look like, if he had grown up." She started to cry.

"I'm sorry for your loss, Mrs. Howard," Steven said.

"He was such a good boy, wasn't he, Alex? I wish . . . oh, I wish . . ." Again, she trailed off.

"He was the best, Mrs. Howard. What do you wish?" Inside, I was screaming. This woman could have helped her son. She could have helped him! Is that why she was broken? From the guilt of knowing she could have saved him?

"Please, call me Sheila. Howard: that was my husband's name."

"What do you wish?"

She got up and started to slowly walk around the room, rearranging an ornament here or there, running her hands over the furniture. "I wish a lot of things, Alex. I wish I could be seeing my boy here, all grown up like you. He never had the chance. His father, my husband, was a very conservative man. He was an angry man, too. He knew how things should go, how things should be.

"I always knew about him, about Taylor." Her face changed when she said his name, and it was a change I could feel, in the goose bumps on my arm, in the pit of my stomach. He was with us, Taylor, in the room with us. More than just a memory. "Well, I suspected. He was a soft boy, a quiet boy. He didn't like to do what the other boys liked to do. Michael, that was my husband's name, he suspected too. He drove Taylor so hard, but the more he drove him, the quieter Taylor became. As Taylor grew up, he learned to say what he had to say and when he had to say it, to appease his father. Things found a balance.

"Here, come with me," she said suddenly, and she walked down the hallway and up the stairs. I looked at Steven, who nodded, and I followed her, with Steven following me, a line of people going farther into the house where Taylor had lived and died, farther into the past. She stopped outside of Taylor's room. I did not want her to open that door. I did not want to see that room. She was standing there with her hand on the doorknob, and she was frozen, as if she too did not want to see that room.

"That night I found you, the two of you, doing what you were doing, I wish I could take it back. I wish I had listened outside this door before I opened it. I wish I hadn't seen what I had seen. I wish you hadn't been doing what you were doing, not when his father was in the house. But wishes won't change what happened." She opened the door.

"I opened the door, and there you were, with him, on him. Do you remember, Alex?"

How could I ever forget? I nodded. She stepped into the room, and I followed. There was his bed, where we had been. The air was musty.

"I didn't mean to say anything. Believe me, I knew what kind of man he was. I didn't mean to say anything. But the words came spilling out and it was too late. He exploded. You were gone already.

That was smart. But he beat Taylor that night; beat him so badly, and when I tried to stop him, he beat me, too. It was my fault, he said, that Taylor was that way.

"But at least when he was beating me, he wasn't beating Taylor. I tried to save my boy that much at least. It was too late, of course. He was already so bruised. I sat there with him, that night, after his father had stormed out of the house. I sat here on this bed, and I stroked my baby boy's hair as he cried himself to sleep.

"I thought maybe it would pass. I thought maybe Taylor would be more careful. I thought maybe my husband would think that the beating had done what he had always said it would do. 'I will beat that boy into a man if I have to,' he had said, so many times. I wish I had listened. I wish I had taken Taylor and run away. I wish so many things."

The words were pouring out of her and ripping into me. My eyes were closed, and I could picture everything as it happened. What had happened after I left. What I had always known had happened. I stood there, Steven's hand on my shoulder. Steven's hand gave me strength. Her words were just words. It didn't matter now. It was in the past.

"What happened next?" Steven asked, and for once, it was me who knew why he said what he said. He knew, and I suddenly knew, too, that she had been waiting to tell this story for thirteen years.

"Taylor went to school the next day. He was wearing this jacket," she said, walking over to the desk and running her hand over the jacket that hung on the back of the chair. I knew that jacket well. I remembered seeing him wrap himself up in it, that last day that I saw him. I remembered the day it had been raining, and I had left my jacket at home, and he loaned me his, even though it meant he got wet. That was the kind of boy he was.

"When he came home, he went right to his room. When his father got home, it happened again. Michael was drunk that night, and that made it worse. He came home, and he went into Taylor's room, and I could hear Taylor scream. The door was locked. I couldn't get in. I tried. Oh, how I tried! I threw myself at the door over and over, and inside, I could hear the thump and thump and thump and scream and scream and scream. And he came out, and pushed me to the floor, and he went to bed. And I lay there, and I could see Taylor on the floor, bruised and bloodied and broken and crying. I crawled over to him, and I held him, there on the floor until he fell asleep. And then I went to bed, next to the man who had done that to him. What else was I supposed to do? I had to hope that was the end.

"It was the end, wasn't it, Alex? The gunshot woke me up, woke both of us up. I jumped from bed, but he just sat up, and said 'good' and rolled over. I found him, in the garage. I will never forget what I saw that night, in the garage. The gun was on the floor where it had flown from him, and he . . ." She was talking fast, and suddenly just stopped.

"I remember seeing you at the funeral, Alex. I didn't know what to say to you. I was angry at you then, for your part in it. I know it wasn't your fault, now, but then, oh, I was angry at you."

"At me? You could have done something!"

"Alex," Steven said. "Stay calm."

"No, he's right. I could have done something. I did do it, too late though. I kicked him out. He worked for my father. I got him fired. I tried to take away from him what he had taken away from me, but how could any house or job compare to my beautiful baby boy? He wore this jacket that day. I left it where he left it. I left everything how he left it."

"I don't know what to say, Mrs. Howard."

"Please, call me Sheila. Here now, we shouldn't be in here. This is Taylor's room. He doesn't like it when I pry. Come boys, let's go back to the living room. I can make us some tea. Would you like some tea? I do enjoy a nice cup of tea."

She walked past us and out the door. Steven looked at me, and then followed her. I took one last look around the room, and then squeezed my eyes shut, capturing the image of this dusty shrine forever. I followed them out and shut the door behind me.

Chapter 42

What should I say? What should I do? I had been carrying around this self-centered assumption that I was the one who was so broken by Taylor's death. This woman, she was the broken one. Thirteen years of living where it happened, of knowing she could have stopped it. Kicking out her husband, getting him fired, they were petty revenges. They were no bandage on the gaping wound that was visible through those haunted eyes.

She made us tea. I had no desire to spend one more second in that house, much less have tea with this woman, but Steven whispered that we couldn't just leave her this soon. I used his phone to call my parents and tell them we'd be later than expected. My phone was still off in the car, and I should check it, but I was in no rush.

We didn't say much of anything as we sipped our tea. What was there to say?

"Is this your boyfriend, Alex?" she said suddenly, and I choked a little on the sip.

"Yes, I am," Steven said, coming to my rescue again. And whether he meant it or not, right then, it meant the world.

"That's nice. You seem like nice boys."

"Thank you," I said, my voice hoarse.

"I wonder if Taylor would have a boy like this. He was a nice boy too."

"Yes, he was, Mrs. . . . Sheila. He was. And he would, indeed." That boy could have been me. Maybe.

"Such a sweet boy, you are. You always were. Here, one second." She put her tea down and walked down the hall. In a minute, she came back, and, cradled in her arms, was Taylor's jacket. She went to hand it to me. "Take this," she said.

I hesitated.

"Please, it would mean so much to me, to know that you have it."

I reached out and touched it. She was holding on to it so tightly, and then let go and turned away. I pulled it close to me. It was impossible, that I could smell him on a jacket from a lifetime before. But holding it, there in that house, I could smell him, taste him, hear him. I could feel him.

"You should go now," she said. "I need to lie down."

"Mrs. Howard, thank you," I said. "Thank you so much."

"You're a polite boy." She walked over to the window and looked out. "He's not coming home, is he?"

"No, Mrs. Howard. He's not."

"No, of course not."

We walked toward the door, and paused as we were about to leave. "Can we do anything for you?" I asked. "Before we go? Or tomorrow?"

"No. I'm fine," she said. "You boys take care." She came toward the door as if to hug us, but only put her hand on the door and started to close it. "Oh, yes, you can do one thing for me, Alex."

"What's that?"

"Never forget my boy."

"Never," I said.

"Good," she said, and closed it a little farther. Her face was only partly visible through the crack when she said, "The happiest he ever was, in his whole life on this earth, was when he was with you."

She closed the door, and I broke down in tears, burying my face in the jacket of the boy I once loved. And then, the man I loved now wrapped his arms around me and led me to the car.

Chapter 43

"Are you okay, Alex?" Steven asked as we drove to my parents' house.

It was a simple question. It was a loaded question. I was sitting there next to my maybe-still-ex-boyfriend, stroking the jacket of my dead-high-school-sweetheart. I had a crazy man sending me pictures of said dead sweetheart, and leaving voice mail for me.

I was far from okay, but I could see okay ahead of me, and maybe not that far ahead. I could see Steven and me working things out, I could see me continuing to choose a different path than cocaine and alcohol. I could see the future I had once dreamed of, still just ahead of me.

"Yeah, I'm okay," I said, and squeezed his hand even as I squeezed Taylor's jacket.

I gave Steven directions, and soon enough, we were there at my parents' house. "What are we telling them?" Steven asked.

"I'd been thinking that same thing myself. Let's keep it light. Mom will worry. We're here to visit some old friends. That's all."

"I'll follow your lead," he said.

"Well, let's go in," I said, and we were no sooner out of the car than my mom was coming down the steps to meet us. Her face lit up and she hugged me. I wrapped my arms around her, my chin on her head. I could smell her shampoo, and it took me back to being a kid, lying next to her on the couch as she read me a book before bed. A simpler time.

"Okay, Alex," she said, her voice muffled in my chest. "You can let go."

We all laughed, and she took us both by the hands and led us inside, where my dad was holding the door open. He clapped his hand on my shoulder as I passed. "Welcome home, son," he said. "And Steven, good to see you, too."

"Come in. Make yourselves at home. Can I get you anything? You ate already? Was the drive good?"

"Slow down, woman," my dad said, laughing. "Can I get you guys a beer?"

Steven looked at me, a raised eyebrow asking my permission. I nodded. "Steven will," I said, "but I'm good."

"I have some wine," my mom said. "I could get you a glass? Here, let me get you a glass."

"No, Mom, I'm good. I've actually decided to stop drinking."

"Oh?" she said, her expression suddenly one of concern.

There was too much to tell her, and no need for her to know it, not if I kept clean and sober. "Don't worry, it's not a big deal. I've just been thinking I want to make some healthier choices. You have your glass of wine though, and Dad, you and Steven have a beer. It's fine."

"Well, if you're sure," Dad said, and he disappeared into the kitchen.

"Is everything okay? What brings you boys to visit? Are you here long?"

"Jesus, Mom, one question at a time," I said with a laugh. That's how she was, a never-ending string of questions and worries and excitement. A little bit dramatic actually. Maybe that's where I got it from, my tendency to feel and react before thinking things through. Her heart was pure, her intentions good, but it was nice, in a non-serious way, to think I could blame her for some of my more . . . theatrical qualities.

We small-talked over drinks, sticking with the we'd-come-to-visit-friends-and-just-for-the-night story we had told them earlier. It was already getting late though, and it had been an exhausting day, physically and emotionally. Steven had barely finished half his beer before I noticed he was starting to doze off.

Mom must have noticed too. "Well, look at us, keeping you guys up talking when you must be tired. Peter, you clean up. I'll just show the boys to their room and then meet you in bed."

"I know where the room is, Mom."

"Now, now, you just let me play gracious hostess. You never come home. Why, this is Steven's first time here, and you've been together a long time. Why, it must be over a year, now."

"A year today," Steven said, stifling a yawn. "But yes, we're pretty beat. Or at least I am. You can stay up, Alex."

"No, I'm done too. Besides," I said to my parents, "don't you guys both work in the morning?"

"Oh, don't you worry about us," Dad said. "We'll be fine. We'll make you guys a nice breakfast before you leave."

"That's not necessary," I said.

"No. It's done," Mom said. "I already took the morning off. Bacon and eggs good enough for you both, I assume? Steven, is there anything you don't like?"

"I'm easy," he said, and it was all I could do not to rise to that bait.

Easy. Yes. That's exactly what things were, right then, right there, between me and Steven. Things were clearer in my head than ever, days removed from alcohol and drugs, and spending all this time together, even under such circumstances, well, it put everything back in perspective. I was a very lucky man, to have found him not only once but twice. Or did this count as the third? If neither a crazy kidnapper nor my drug-induced drama could keep us apart, then that was a pretty strong sign that this was meant to be.

"Alex?" he said, pulling me from my thoughts. "Are you coming to bed?"

He pulled me up from the couch, and we hugged my parents good night. Mom insisted on walking us to our room, and kissing us both again at the door. "If you need blankets, there's some in the closet. We'll see you boys in the morning."

She opened the door for us and we stepped into the room as she turned on the light. She smiled, a smile that was warm and knowing and still a little bit sad, as she pulled the door closed behind her. And there we were.

This wasn't the room I had grown up in. My parents had sold that house. But it felt like it could have been. Even though there was nothing of my teenage years around, not like the shrine that Taylor's mom had, I suddenly felt very weird. I had a boy in my room. With my parents in the house.

Was that a feeling anyone ever outgrew?

I looked at Steven, and he was standing there, uncomfortable, and blushing a bit. I guess he was feeling it too. I smiled at him.

"Shut up," he said, playfully punching my arm. It was nice to know that as much as he could read my mind, I could read his as well. Sometimes. "Let's go to bed."

I sat down on the bed and pulled off my pants. Without even looking, I could sense Steven behind me, standing there, unbuttoning his shirt. I was suddenly all nervous. My hands were sweating. We had spent many nights in bed together. We had definitely seen each other naked. Why was I all blushing-virgin-bride all of a sudden?

"Can I get the lights?"

I turned, and Steven was standing there in his briefs (perfectly packaged), his hand on the switch.

"Yes," I said, and the room was plunged into darkness. I quickly finished undressing, leaving my undies on too. I heard Steven cross the room, fumbling his way back to the bed, swearing as he bumped into the footboard. We crawled under the covers and I lay there, staring into the blackness above, my arms at my sides, him next to me, his arms at his sides.

"I . . ."

"I . . ." We both spoke at the same time and started to laugh.

"You go first," he said.

"No, you."

"Alex, just say it." His hand found mine, on the sheets between our bodies. His fingers intertwined mine.

"I just wanted to say thanks."

"For what?"

"For everything. I don't know. For being you."

"You're welcome, Alex."

We lay there. He stroked my hand with his thumb. "What did you want to say?" I asked.

"Sorry?"

"You were going to say something too."

"Oh. Just . . ." I felt him shift next to me as he propped himself up on his elbow. "I love you."

He leaned down and found my lips in the dark. Everything was right.

He was calling to me.

I couldn't see him.

The room was filled with people. Wonderland always was. There was no music though. Just people everywhere, milling around. I was standing there, in the middle of the crowd of generic, faceless people.

"Alex," he called again.

"Steven?" I called out.

"Alex!"

And there he was, bobbing up and down above the crowd, waving his hands above his head.

"Steven!"

The room zoomed out, and more people came flooding in as the bar expanded. He kept getting farther and farther away, and I could barely see him anymore. Just a head among the heads. I couldn't hear him now. There was a drone of people talking, gossiping, laughing, crying, His head disappeared, and it was just fingertips above the crowd. And then that was gone too.

Steven was gone.

Chapter 44

When I woke up, Steven was gone. I hadn't heard him get out of bed, hadn't even felt him get out. I wandered downstairs, and found Mom making breakfast.

"Have you seen Steven?" I asked.

"Morning to you, too, dear. How did you sleep? Can I get you some coffee, or some juice?"

I blushed. "Sorry, morning, Mom." And I kissed her cheek. "Now, have you seen him?"

She laughed as she poured me some juice, and suddenly I was ten again, and late for school. Except if I had been ten, I'd have been waiting for Nathan. We were inseparable then.

"He went for a run. He said to eat without him."

Steven and his runs. He could be gone for an hour or two. The man loved to jog. And had the body to show for it. A fact I appreciated immensely, I thought, as I scooped out a heaping plate of bacon and eggs. Me, I wasn't so big on the running. Luckily, my metabolism was still working in my favor. I was thirty though. That was bound to change.

"You'll be good here, if I leave?" Mom asked. "I would stay and visit but I have some stuff I really should get done before work. You'll be okay? Lock up before you guys hit the road? Come by the store and say good-bye?"

"Yes, Mother."

She kissed me on the cheek. "It was so good seeing you guys. You need to come visit more often. Your dad and I, we worry about you too. Since . . . well, since everything that happened. We are so happy to see that everything is working out now though."

After she left, her words weighed heavily on my guilty heart. I hadn't lied. Not really. Evaded, omitted, but not lied. But she was my mom. Didn't that mean she deserved to know the truth? The truth. Sex. Drugs. Breakups. Harassment. She was my mom. I couldn't tell her those things. The despair and disappointment on her face if I ever did would be more than I could handle.

It occurred to me suddenly that I hadn't checked my phone for a while. Not since I'd sent out the message with my new number to everyone, to Aaron. While Steven was running, maybe I should stop running, stop hiding. Turning off my phone had been a pretty chickenshit thing to do, easier than sitting there waiting for them not to reply.

I took my coffee and my phone out onto the deck overlooking the backyard. Living in the gayborhood was great, the condos rising above the world. But I missed the simple things, like coffee on a deck. Steven had a deck. I loved sitting on Steven's deck.

Jesus, Alex, I thought, that doesn't sound right.

I turned my iPhone over and over in my hands, and then powered it up. For a moment, I wondered whether I wanted there to be messages or not, but then they began to roll in, and for good or bad, they were there.

MWAH. Loads of love—from Dinah.

Thanks Alex. Hope you're well—from Colton.

Should I pass this on to Allan so he can fuck you again? LOSE MY NUMBER—from Brandon.

Does this mean you're done being a douche?—from Jesse.

SERIOUSLY LOSE MY NUMBER—from Brandon again.

Hey thanks I am glad you're sober and I am glad you're doing better and I'm glad you gave me your new number. I'm sorry for everything that happened and I miss you. Just as a friend. I enjoyed having you back in my life. Let's do coffee?—from Aaron.

OK, I talked to Jesse and Colton and I guess we're done being mad at you and that you're seriously trying to get your shit together so you don't need to lose my number but seriously, Alex, don't fuck up again—from Brandon.

They like me, I thought. They really like me.

I sent a simple **xo** to Dinah and Colton and a **yes yes it does** to Jesse. To Brandon, I sent **I swear. No more fuckups. No more drama. No more anything.**

And that left Aaron.

Coffee would be good. I'm out of town right now. Should be back soon. Maybe this weekend?

He replied almost right away. **Where are you?**

At my parents'.

What's that about?

Where to even start, I thought. **Steven and I came to visit. I wanted to get out of the city.** That was innocuous enough.

You and Steven, hey? Are you guys working things out then?

I think so.

Nothing ever happened with us, Alex. Well, ok, yes, that one thing happened between us, but not what you thought.

I know.

He loves you.

I know that too.

So we can do coffee?

Yeah. I'll call when we're back.

Sounds good.

No three-ways though, I typed, smiling, and realized that just like that, if I could joke about it, it was done. Oh no. There it was. The picture of them kissing, back in my head, twisting in my heart. No! I wouldn't let myself think that again. It was over and done with. Steven and I were moving on, and the past was in the past. I had to let it go.

My interior monologue was getting increasingly gay, I thought, from Sally Field to *Frozen* in just a few text messages. Steven would appreciate it. He loved Disney movies. Every Tuesday, we would order in Chinese and watch an animated classic. We had to do it again. And soon.

Where was Steven? He should be back by now.

How are you doing though, really? Aaron texted. **I know about the graffiti and Allan.**

Of course he did. **Things are fucked up. But they're getting better. Steven's helping.**

And being sober helps too, I am sure.

That it does. I paused. **How is life for you?**

Life's good. Work. You know.

Anything new?

Wonderland wants me to do a onetime comeback special.

I smiled. The realization that Aaron had been Wonderland's star entertainer, the Queen of Hearts, had been lost in the confusion and chaos surrounding Steven's kidnapping. But he had retired from drag, the shortest career in the spotlight ever. He had been good though. So very very good.

Are you going to do it? You should.

I probably am. It's a cancer fundraiser.

Aaron had lost both his parents to cancer. That cause would be all it took for him to brush off his heels again. The first time Steven had said he loved me had been at a Queen of Hearts show.

Seriously, where was Steven?

I sent him a text **do you have your phone with you? Are you almost done?**

The message showed *delivered* but sat there, unread. Maybe he had that feature turned off. No. He never turned it off. Oh well, he was probably just enjoying his run. He hadn't gone for a couple of days.

I hopped in the shower, and when I was done, and he still wasn't back, I cleaned up the kitchen a bit for Mom (not that she had left much of anything for me to do). Dinah and I texted back and forth a bit more. She was giddy with excitement about the pregnancy, and very glad that the wedding would be before she got too big. Was it really only a month away? Time flew by when you were flying high.

After an hour, I called Steven. The phone rang and rang and went to voice mail. Maybe he hadn't taken it, I thought, and checked our room, and then inside the car. No. He definitely had it on him. It had all his music on it. He never ran without music. Why wasn't he answering?

It was just a feeling in the pit of my stomach, and I knew it was just because of before, because of what happened with Nathan. Of course he was fine. He was just running. Nothing had happened. There was no need for this paranoia.

But it had been a couple hours. Not unheard of if he got into a zone. But where around here would he have gone for that long of a run?

I figured I'd go for a walk, see if I could find him. The fresh air would do me good anyway. God knows I had spent enough time indoors without any exercise or sunshine.

How's the parents? Aaron asked.

Same as always. They never change.

What are you guys doing?

Well, right now, actually, I'm going for a walk. Steven's been out running for a couple hours. I'm curious where he's gotten to.

Probably just got carried away. You know how he is on his runs.

I did know how he is on his runs. And I had to yell at my brain to be quiet about Aaron knowing that too. We had been friends, all three of us, for the brief window between kidnapping and threesome. That was all. It meant nothing.

I went down the block, heading toward the river valley. That's where Steven would have gone. He loved that river. This same river wound its way along the freeway, back to the city, our city, past our secret special spot. If you kept following the river, eventually, a few hours south and east, you'd get to Steven's parents' town. He had spent his whole life by the river.

Steven? I texted again, though the other messages still showed up as unread.

I started walking faster when more time passed with no answer. Something was wrong. Had he fallen? Was he hurt? Did he twist an ankle, or maybe get lost?

I think something's wrong, I texted Aaron. **It's been like three hours now.**

That's a bit much, even for Steven.

I don't know where to look though.

Don't panic. He's fine.

That's what I wanted to believe. That's what I kept telling myself. That wasn't enough to stop the voice inside my head from saying over and over again the thing I didn't want to believe: that yet again, Steven was missing.

Chapter 45

It couldn't be.

Not again.

Alex, you're being paranoid.

Think.

Where else could he have gone? You're just randomly hoping to run into him. He's probably at the house, waiting for you, wondering where you've gotten to.

That was it.

That had to be it.

I did an about-face and headed back home, steady, and then faster and faster. I was running, racing back to my parents', where Steven would be.

Where Steven had to be.

Nathan was the one who had tried to hurt him.

Nathan was locked up.

Steven was safe.

But the picture. The calls. Someone was messing with me.

And Steven going missing, again, that would mess with me in a big way. A huge way. A call-the-Caterpillar way.

Steven could not be missing.

Steven would not be missing.

But when I got back to the house, there was no Steven.

And it was coming up on four hours now.

I tried calling again, but there was no answer, again.

And then it occurred to me.

Oh wonderful Apple with your wonderful iPhones, and more importantly, your wonderful find-your-iPhone technology!

When I got Steven back the last time, we had realized how much we never wanted something like that to happen again. Steven had told me his Apple ID so I could trace his iPhone. Just in case. Not that lightning ever struck twice. But just in case.

How did I forget?

I logged into his account and activated the feature, and there he was! Just blocks away!

A wave of relief passed over me as I headed to find him, and the panic and paranoia fled from me in a nervous laugh. What an idiot, I thought. What were the chances really, of Steven going missing, twice in one year? It was ludicrous, laughable, and laugh we would, right away, as soon as I found him.

According to the app, I was nearly there.

And then there I was, and it showed him, right there. But I looked around and couldn't see him. I was at the end of a road, and traffic passed by me, standing there stupefied on the corner. Was he in a passing car? No. He was right at this intersection.

Except he wasn't.

I tried calling again, and I heard it ring.

I spun around. He had to be right here!

It went to voice mail, and I called again. Ring. Ring. It was getting louder. Ring. What the . . .

And there it was. Steven's phone. Just lying there against the curb. In the street. Without Steven. His earbuds were still attached.

Panic rushed back in.

This wasn't right. This wasn't right at all.

I picked it up and looked around. Where was he? What had happened?

I called Aaron automatically. "He's gone," I said as soon as he picked up the phone.

"What?"

"Steven. He's gone. Again. He's gone. I can't believe it."

"Slow down, Alex. What do you mean he's gone?"

"I found his phone, just lying in the street. He's missing. What am I gonna do, Aaron? I can't go through this again."

"Calm down. Where are you?"

"A few blocks from my parents' house. It's like he just vanished into thin air."

"Okay, I want you to take a deep breath. You're going to hang up the phone and call the police. No messing around this time, okay? Just call them right away."

"Okay. I will." My eyes were hot and heavy with tears I wouldn't let fall as my chest heaved with panic.

"When you get off the phone with the police, you call me back immediately, okay?"

"Okay. I will."

"Promise?"

"I promise. I'll call you as soon as I talk to the police. Tell me he'll be fine."

"Of course he's fine."

"Promise?"

"Promise. Now call them."

"Okay. Thank you, Aaron. I . . . I know I could have called anyone, but . . ."

"Hush, you. I know. Call the police, Alex."

"I'm calling them now."

I hung up the phone and closed my eyes, trying to calm my breathing. My hands were shaking and sweaty. God, what if . . . how could he . . . So many thoughts ran through my head. I just needed to breathe.

"Call the police, Alex," I told myself out loud. "No messing around this time." The phone slipped from my hand. "Fuck."

As I bent down to pick it up, I felt him behind me.

"You won't need the phone, Alex."

I knew the voice immediately. From the phone. From the voice mails. I spun around, and saw a man standing there, gray hair, gray scruff, gray skin, gray coat. I knew him though, I thought, as he took a step toward me and reached into his coat pocket. He pulled out a gun and held it to my side.

"Don't make a noise, Alex. Not one fucking noise."

"Who . . . why . . ."

"Come with me," he said.

He jabbed the gun into my side. Into my right side. In my left hand, I suddenly realized, I had Steven's phone. I glanced at my phone, on the sidewalk. His gray eyes followed mine.

"Oh no," he said, swooping down to pick it up. While he did, I dialled 911 with Steven's phone, but as he came back up, he saw it in my hand.

"Not quite, faggot," he said, grabbing both phones and tossing them through a sewer grate in the road. "Nice try though, but no."

He pressed himself up against me, his hand clamping the back of my neck like we were friends, or lovers. "This way," he said, and he squeezed tightly on my neck as he pulled me up the walk to a house. A normal house, in a normal neighborhood. He stank of booze as he pulled me up the steps to the front door. "Get inside," he said, opening the door and pushing me in. I saw him glance up and down the street quickly before he came in and closed the door behind him.

He pointed with the gun into the next room. "Welcome, Alex," he said.

It was a normal living room in a normal house in a normal neighborhood, but it was anything but normal. Who was he? His face was screaming in my head for recognition. I knew him.

"I have waited so long for this day," he said. "For the day a murderer like you gets justice."

Murderer? And suddenly I knew. I saw the picture of Taylor (*You killed me*). Taylor, with those playful loving eyes. Almost the same eyes that looked at me now.

"Mr. Howard?" The words came as a croak.

"Bingo, faggot," he said. "Are you ready to die?" He raised the gun.

Chapter 46

"Alex!"

Steven's voice pierced me and I jumped away from Mr. Howard.

"Oh no," he said, grabbing hold of me. He was strong, much stronger than he looked. I strained against him as he wrapped his arm around my chest.

"Steven!" I screamed back.

"Shut up!" Mr. Howard said. "Shut up, or you'll die right now and never see him again. Is that what you want? To never see him again?"

"Just let us go," I said.

"No. You don't get to walk away from this. You need to pay for what you did."

"What did I do? I didn't do anything. Taylor killed . . ."

I didn't see the blow coming. My head was suddenly just exploding with pain and my vision was red, and my knees gave out under me.

"Shut your fucking queer mouth! Shut it! Shut it!"

He pulled me to my feet and shoved me in front of him, toward a closed door. He opened it, and pushed me through. "Get down!" he said, pointing toward the stairs with the gun. "Down!"

Reeling from the pain, I stumbled down, blinking away tears. I stumbled the last few stairs.

"Alex!"

There was Steven, and I had seen this scene before. He was bound to a chair and he was straining against the ropes, and I saw it so clearly, what I had seen before, when I had burst in on Nathan. "Alex!" Steven called to me now, like he had done then.

Mr. Howard threw me to the floor. "Well, then, here we are. And this is how it will finally end. After all these years."

"What are you doing? What are you talking about?"

"You know what you did, Alex. You took my boy and changed him into something like you. A sick perversion. He didn't want to be that way. He was strong, at the end. I made him strong. I beat him until he was man enough to end it all. He died a man."

I lay there on the floor as he talked, too scared to move. His eyes were wild, his eyes, Taylor's eyes. I could hear Steven whimpering as he strained against the ropes that bound him.

"Let Steven go," I said. "This has nothing to do with him. He didn't even know Taylor."

"Do not say his name! He was my son, and you twisted him. He was always a soft boy, but he never would have become . . . like you, if you hadn't made him. You killed him, Alex, surely as if you had pulled the trigger yourself. Does that make you feel happy? His blood is on your hands."

"Well then, just shoot me. If that's what you're going to do, just be done with it."

"No, no, no. You need to suffer like I have suffered. You didn't just take my boy away, you took my whole life away. That bitch, his mother, and her fucking father took away my job, my livelihood, my future. I have waited for this chance for years. You can wait now." He waved the gun at me. "Onto your stomach," he said.

"Why?"

"Do it!" his voice boomed.

Trembling, I did what he said. What choice did I have? Should I tell him that all that had happened was because of him, not me? I hadn't done that. His hatred had taken it all away from him. His actions. His words. Words had power. I was seeing that now, but only if you let them. Words like *faggot.* It only hurt if you let it hurt. He chose words that hurt, that hurt Taylor, that hurt Sheila, that hurt himself. I was choosing other words, hopeful words. Loving words. But should I use those words here? Was there a point? I didn't even care what happened to me. I just wanted Steven free. Maybe if I did what he said, he would let Steven go. That's all that mattered.

He pulled a box across the concrete and took a rope from it. "You will wait like I have waited," he said. He wrapped the rope around my feet and tightened it. I could feel it biting into my legs as he pulled the knots tighter and tighter.

"Why now?"

"I saw you," he said. "After so many years of only seeing you in my head, seeing you and hating you, there you were on the TV. Oh, how I wish that other useless kid had done it properly. But oh no, you escaped, you and this other faggot here, and I knew if I wanted it done, I had to do it myself. A man does it himself. At first, I thought it would be enough to drive you crazy. Some paint on your door. The picture. The phone calls. I watched you, saw you unraveling. But it wasn't enough." He climbed up on top of me and pulled my arms behind my back and began to secure them with another piece of rope. "I followed you," he explained. "To the prison. Around the city. I followed you back here. I knew this was my chance. When I saw this one running, I knew you would come looking for him. Like you did before." I groaned under him. "That should hold you until it's time," he said.

"Time for what?"

He leaned down against me, and then pulled my hair as he breathed into my ear. "Time for you to die." He spit in my face and then ground my face down into the floor. I screamed. "You can't get out," he said. "These knots are tight. Don't even try."

"If I don't try, will you let Steven go?"

"He means a lot to you? This other faggot? He means a lot to you?"

"Yes! Please! Just let him go. He won't go to the police. Just let him go."

"If he means so much to you, you can watch him die first. I'll shoot him in the head, just like you did to Taylor."

"No!"

Mr. Howard got off me. "I'll be back," he said. "I need a drink."

He walked up the stairs and I lifted my head to watch as he disappeared. The room plunged into darkness and I heard the door close. I struggled against the ropes but he was right. They were too tight.

"Alex, Alex, are you okay?"

"Steven!" I called out and flopped around on the floor so I was facing in his direction. It was dark. The one window, high up the walls, was blocked by weeds from outside, and the light it did let in was barely enough for me to see Steven, his shape there. "Oh God, Steven. I am so sorry. Are you okay? What did he do to you?"

"Nothing," he said. "I was running and he stopped me and asked me for help with a piece of furniture. When we came inside, he pulled the gun on me. But I'm not hurt. I can't get undone though."

"Me either. Oh Steve, please believe me, I'm sorry."

"Stop apologizing. This isn't your fault. He's insane."

I let out a brief, hysterical laugh. "But again, it's someone insane from my past, and you're in danger because of it."

"We'll get out," he said. "We escaped Nathan. We can escape this guy. At least this time, we're together."

"Let me see if I can get over to you. Maybe we can get out."

"Be careful."

I flopped again and laughed nervously, thinking how I must look like a fish out of water. I moved maybe half an inch. Maybe. Steven was a good four feet away. Strain. Flop. Strain. Flop. Jump. Flop. Strain.

I was sore and sweating and had barely moved.

"Can you get closer?"

"I tried moving before. The chair is too heavy."

"Fuck! What are we going to do?" Strain. Flop. Jump.

"Calm down, Alex. He'll slip up. We'll find a way."

"If only I had been able to call the police first. But he stopped me before I could."

"Do you still have the phone?"

"He threw them both away."

"Fuck. Oh well, next plan."

"Maybe Aaron will call them."

"Aaron?"

"He knows you're missing. I called him when I found your phone. He is expecting me to call him back after I talk to the police."

Strain. Flop. Jump. Another half inch.

"I love you, Steven."

"I love you, too. You know that."

A bit more. A bit more.

"If we don't get out of this . . ." I started.

"We will," he said.

"I know, but if we don't . . ."

"There is no if."

"Just let me say it."

"Okay."

"If we don't get out of this, I want you to know that I have never been so happy as when I was with you." Another inch closer to Steven. His foot was just a couple feet away from my face.

"Alex, shhhh. You don't need to tell me stuff I know."

"But I . . ."

"When we get out of this, I'm putting the ring back on."

"What?"

"You heard me."

"Do you mean it though? I'm such a mess."

"You're better now. It's been days. You've hit rock bottom and you're climbing back up, and I will be there every step of the way."

In spite of everything, I felt so happy and proud right then. It warmed me up, made me forget that I was flopping across the floor in a psychopath's dark basement. Well, maybe not forget. But it distracted me. For a minute. And then back to the strain, flop, jump. Another half inch. All I had to do was get to Steven. If I could just touch him, just be in contact with him, we would figure this out.

Another half inch . . .

Chapter 47

How long I struggled to get across the floor to Steven, I don't know. I was nearly there, though. My eyes were adjusted to the dark, and there was just enough light coming through the one window for me to make out Steven's face. His eyes were on me, never left me, and as he strained against his ropes, I jumped and flopped another half inch.

And another.

And then the door opened and the lights came on, and hope turned to bitter disappointment. I looked around quickly, as Mr. Howard stumbled down the stairs, a bottle of Jack Daniel's in one hand. There had to be something that could help us. Boxes filled with junk were piled up against the walls. A ratty old couch. Some tools on a shelf. Yes, maybe if I could get there, but it was behind Steven, and I couldn't even get to him.

"Slithering across the floor like a worm," Mr. Howard said, slurring his words. He had had more than one drink, that was for sure. The smell stuck to him, strong and overpowering, and sweet. I felt my body crave it, whiskey instead of gin, sure, but the same amazing oblivion.

He lurched toward Steven, past me. Where was the gun? I couldn't see it. Would he pass out? Would that be the chance we needed? "Here, faggot. Drink." He pulled Steven's head back by the hair and poured the whiskey into his mouth. Steven sputtered, choked, coughed.

"And now you," he said to me, and he knelt down next to me, and grabbed hold of my hair.

I closed my lips tightly. I couldn't drink. Yes, it had been thirsty work, but nothing compared to the work of being sober these past few days. I wouldn't let him.

"Drink!" he said.

He squeezed my cheeks, forcing my lips open. I squirmed and flailed but he poured it over my mouth, warm and wet and strong. I felt it run down my throat and fill my chest, glowing, burning its way through me.

He pushed me back to the floor and sat down on the couch, taking a long swig from the bottle. "You saw my wife," he said, and it wasn't a question. He had been watching. What had he seen? What did he know? And what did he want?

"Yes." He was calmer now than before. Maybe if I kept him talking . . .

"That crazy cunt. Still there, in that house, waiting for her faggot son to come home. She's fucking loony tunes, I'll tell you that. But you know. You saw her. You went in." He looked at me. "What did she give you? I saw you come out with something."

"His jacket." There was no point in lying. Not anymore. Not about something like that.

He took another drink. The bottle was three quarters gone. "A jacket. She didn't even let me have that much when she kicked me out. Her and that old man of hers. The clothes on my back, that was it. Drove me out of my own home! Out of my job, at a company I had slaved away at for twenty years. Who the fuck do they think they are?"

"I'm sorry that happened to you," Steven said, and I knew he had the same thought as me. Keeping him talking gave us time.

"Shut up. You're not in this. Not really. Only because you matter to him. He needs to pay." He drank down another gulp. "You hear that, Alex? You're going to pay. You took Taylor, and then they took everything else. None of it was my fault, but I was the one who suffered."

"We can't help what happened," Steven said.

"Shut your fucking faggot mouth. I told you, you're not in this." He reached behind him and pulled the gun out from the waistband of his pants. He took another drink. "Just stay quiet. You'll die fast. Taylor died fast." He closed his eyes and his head swayed a little. Was he falling asleep? Was he so drunk already that he was ready to pass out? His eyes popped open again. "It was the only masculine thing he ever did in his life. She made him soft. You made him queer. The world. It's bad to be a man now. But he was a man then. For that one moment. He blew his fucking brains out. Just like I am going to do to you." He waved the gun at Steven and I screamed out.

"Oh, you too, Alex. You too. For sure, you too. But you're going to watch him die first. You're going to watch as the thing that matters to you goes away. Like I had to do. Not the queer son or the crazy cunt wife. But the life I had built for myself. It all went away. Now there's this," he said, waving the bottle of Jack, "and this," he added, waving the gun. "And revenge. Always revenge."

"But you know it wasn't my fault," I said. "I didn't do anything to Taylor."

"You did!" He lurched to his feet, and then slumped back into the cushions of the couch. "You did! She saw you together. She saw exactly what you were doing to him. She told me, and she knew how I would react. She had no one to blame for what happened. Of course I beat him fucking senseless. It's wrong, and no son of mine . . ." He closed his eyes again. "No son of mine was going to be that way. 'Better off dead,' I told her. 'Better off dead,' I told him, as I was hitting him. 'You'd be better off dead than a faggot,' I said, and I hit him. And he agreed with me. I am his father. I am the law. He knew that." He yawned. "He knew that . . ." His head hit his chest.

Was he asleep? I looked at Steven, and he shook his head. Don't take a chance, he was saying. Just wait it out, he was urging.

But no. I couldn't just do that. I had to try. Strain. Jump. Flop. Closer to Steven. Closer to the couch. Closer. Closer. Closer.

I kept my eyes on Mr. Howard, as I kept at it. I could feel Steven watching me, begging me with his look to just wait for the right chance. I refused to think about what would happen if I did get to him. How would it help? How would we escape? We would figure that out then. I just had to get to him. Just had to touch him. Strain. Jump. Flop.

I rolled, and felt my leg bump into Mr. Howard's foot. He stirred, made a sound. I froze. Would he wake? Was this it? I lifted my head as high as I could. I could see the gun in his open hand. If I could just get untied, I could take it. But no. Untied was easier said than done. The struggle across the floor was tightening the ropes that bound me.

Strain. Jump. Flop.

My eyes were on Steven. He was so close. So very close. Just a bit more straining, a bit more jumping, a bit more flopping. I'd be there. And then . . .

And then what, Alex? I thought. So we were touching. We'd still be bound. We still couldn't do anything. And any second, the father of my dead high school boyfriend would wake up and . . . No. I couldn't think about what might happen. Only what I had to do.

I landed too hard on my shoulder and couldn't help but grunt.

"Whaaaaa . . . ?"

Mr. Howard sat upright and I felt the hope crumble in my chest.

"Trying to escape?" He lurched to his feet, and took a giant swig of Jack. "You sad pathetic little faggot. There's no escape."

He pointed the gun at Steven and fired.

Chapter 48

I screamed in disbelief as the kickback knocked Mr. Howard onto the couch. It was so fast—well, it was a bullet so of course it was fast—but it was still eerily slow motion. I saw him fall back in the couch even as I struggled toward Steven.

The noise he made when the bullet hit him (in the chest? the shoulder? I couldn't tell), I will never forget. It was a scream and a grunt and then a moan of indescribable pain. He jerked in the chair and the white T-shirt he always wore running was suddenly bright red.

There was so much blood.

Steven's blood.

"Steven!" I screamed out.

In even slower motion, the chair fell over, taking him down to the floor, his mouth open, his face white, his shirt redder and redder and redder.

I didn't have to hear his breath gurgling out of him to know.

Steven was dying.

I saw him getting into his white Rabbit, in the parking lot so long ago. A year and a day ago, I guessed. I saw him running out of his house, a short while later, waving his fists in the air after I had accidentally backed into his car. I saw him across the table from me, smiling coyly, as we had dinner that night.

Steven was dying.

I saw him, in our special, secret spot by the river, where we sat and looked up at the clouds and told each other all our deepest longings. I saw him at Wonderland, at the Queen of Hearts show, where he leaned across the table and told me he loved me. I saw him in bed later that night, above me, in me, around me.

Steven was dying.

I saw him, beaten and broken and bruised, tied to that chair in Nathan's dingy apartment. I saw the joy on his face when he saw me there, finally. I saw the relief on his face when Nathan lay there, shot and bleeding, and we were free.

And now Steven lay there shot and bleeding.

Steven was dying.

I knew it.

There was so much blood.

I saw him in bed with Aaron and felt all that self-loathing and jealousy all over again. I saw the contempt on his face when he saw me at Dinah's bachelorette party. I saw the disappointment in his face when I pulled out the cocaine in front of him. I saw the pride in his face when I threw it out.

Steven was dying.

I saw Steven, and in every image of every memory that flashed through my head, the good, the bad, the beautiful, the tragic, I saw his eyes, and his eyes never changed. They would see me seeing him, and they would glow, warm and rich and filled with love. I saw Steven loving me.

And now I saw Steven dying.

And there was nothing I could do.

Chapter 49

"He doesn't die so pretty, does he?"

Mr. Howard was standing over me, and a thick ball of Jack Daniel's spit fell onto my face.

"You sick fucking monster!" I tried to stand but couldn't. "Steven!"

"You want to say your good-byes?" He pulled my hair, dragged me over to Steven, threw my face onto his chest. His blood was warm and wet and sticky. And red, so very red.

"I guess it doesn't matter if you get it on you. You already have whatever is in it. Keep that fucking faggot blood off me, though."

"Shut up!" I looked up, but all I could see was the swell of his chest, heaving and red, and his chin, stubbled and perfect. "Steven, Steven, you'll be okay."

"Alex . . ."

His voice was barely audible.

"Don't worry, Alex. It won't be long. He'll die. And then you'll die."

"Shut up!" I screamed, and I sat up, fierce and fast, and felt more than saw Steven's blood go flying off my face.

"What the . . ."

I looked up, to see Mr. Howard wiping the blood off him.

"Faggot!" He kicked me in the stomach and I doubled over. "You got his fucking faggot blood on me! Who knows what you gave me, you stupid piece of faggot shit? His diseased fucking blood."

"You stop it!"

I looked up and saw Sheila standing there. How . . . Why . . .

"What the fuck are you doing here, you stupid cunt?"

"Stop it, Michael. Stop it right now."

"He got his faggot blood on me."

"Stop it!" She ran down the stairs. "Stop it!"

"I warned you, bitch." He took a step toward her, the gun in his hand.

"That's the same," she said. "The same as Taylor's blood. Stop it! This won't happen again. I won't let you kill another one."

"What the fuck are you talking about? I didn't kill anyone."

"You beat him until he had no choice! You did it, Michael! You!"

I saw his fist coming before she did. "Sheila!" I called out.

"What's happening?" Steven asked.

Sheila shrieked as his fist hit her. She went stumbling backward, crashing into the shelves on the wall. "I should have killed you," he said.

"Please, stop!" I yelled.

He spun on me, his eyes wide and wild. "Oh, I haven't forgotten you," he said. "This is all on you, Alex. All on you. Everything started to fall apart when you came along. With your filthy faggotry. You destroyed my life. You took my home, my job, my son . . ."

"I didn't! I did nothing! You did it! I loved your son, you twisted hateful bastard! You're the piece of shit who beat him until he had no choice but to put a bullet through his own head!"

"Shut up! It wasn't me! You made him that way!" He raised the gun. I closed my eyes. This was it. "You! It was you! It was . . ."

"No!"

I opened my eyes in time to see Sheila take a few fast steps toward him, a board in her hand.

"What . . ." he said, and turned to face her, and then . . .

Thwack!

He dropped to the floor.

Thwack!

She hit him again.

And again. *Thwack!*

And again. *Thwack!*

And then she dropped to her knees, crying, blood streaming down her face.

She was sobbing, heaving.

"Sheila . . ."

"What? Oh! Alex! Here, let me help you!"

"No, please help Steven."

"What? Oh. Yes. Of course." She got to her feet, wobbling a bit, then turned and headed up the stairs. "I'll call for an ambulance."

"Alex . . ."

"Don't talk, Steven. She's gone to get help."

Why hadn't I gotten her to untie me first? Or the gun! What if he came to? What if . . .

"Alex . . ."

"What is it, Steven? Save your strength. Don't talk."

"I love you . . ."

"Don't! Don't you dare say good-bye."

"It's dark."

Oh God, no. Please please please God. Let him be okay. I needed him. Why did I only know how much now when I was losing him?

"They're coming, Steven. Help is coming. Just hold on." I could feel him shudder.

"They're coming." Sheila came running back down the stairs. "They're coming."

"The gun! Sheila! Please, get the gun!"

She stopped at Michael's body, looking down at it. The man who was once her husband. The man who had fathered her son. The man who had beaten them both. She leaned down, and rolled the body over to get at the gun.

It was clear she didn't need to, though. The impact of the board had smashed in his face.

It was over.

He was dead.

Chapter 50

"How?" I asked Sheila. "I don't even. . . . How are you here? Why?"

Tears fell from my face. Steven lay bleeding on the floor and I couldn't hear the sirens that meant help was here. That Taylor's dad had come lurching from the past, to take from me the man I loved. Again. First Taylor, now Steven.

"How did you know?"

"He sent me this," she said, pulling a piece of paper from her pants pocket. She handed it to me. "It was in an envelope filled with pictures of you, and newspaper clippings from when that other man attacked you."

I opened the letter.

> *I have found him. The faggot who killed your son. He's going to pay for what he did. I have been waiting for this. I have been following him, and one day soon, he is going to pay for what he did. That's when it all went wrong. First him, then you. I will finish what I should have done a long long time ago, you stupid bitch.*

"He sent this to you?"

"Yes. I came to tell him to leave me alone. That I would go to the police. Over the years, he has sent me others. Drunken, hate-filled ramblings, but this, it was different. This time, I could tell he meant it. If I hadn't come when I did . . ."

"But you did."

"I'm glad."

"Me too. Thank you." *Even if it was too late for Steven*, I thought. He was still breathing though. So much blood. Where was the ambulance? Where were the police? "Thank you."

"I couldn't let him do it again, you see. He's to blame, for what happened to my son. For what he did to himself. What Michael made him do. Not again. If he came for me, it didn't matter. I am to blame to, for what happened. But not you. Not you, Alex. Never you." She took my hand in hers. It was sweaty, and her eyes locked with mine, and they were wide and sad. "I never blamed you for Taylor dying."

She started to sob, and I could feel the tears on my cheeks. Taylor was gone, and Steven was going.

Suddenly, I heard the sound of approaching sirens. "Steven!" I leaned down to his ear. "They're here. Hold on. They're here."

Chapter 51

Sunday brunch at the Duchess was a tradition, but it was a tradition that was ending. Steven and I went there together, hand in hand, the Sunday after what happened in that basement. There was a sign on the door saying that the Duchess would be closing at the end of the month. The building was getting torn down to make way for another condo-in-the-sky, and the gayborhood would never be the same.

Neither would we.

When his bandages came off, Steven would have a scar from the bullet, but no other permanent damage. How he survived, I had no idea, but every second of every day for the rest of my life, I would be grateful he did. And I would be grateful for Sheila, for showing up like she did and saving us.

When the ambulance came for Steven, the police came too, with their questions about what had happened. How he had harassed me, assaulted us, shot Steven. How Sheila had had no choice but to hit him with that board.

Thank God she had.

If she hadn't . . .

But she had.

And that was all that mattered.

That, and that Steven was wearing the ring again.

That, and that I was now almost a week clean and sober.

Nothing else mattered. No what-ifs. No could-have-happeneds.

It didn't really even matter that the Duchess was closing.

"Except it kinda does," Steven said, when I mentioned that.

"Why?"

"I always wanted them to cater my wedding," he said, with a smile. "Our wedding." His smile got bigger, as did mine.

"Why all grins, boys?"

It was Aaron, walking across the room to join us. "Not that you don't both have cause to be happy. I am just amazed . . ."

"Us too."

He had called the police, too, when I hadn't called him back. They had gone to my parents', but there wasn't much they could do at that point. I was grateful he had, though.

He sat down. "Are we having mimosas?"

"I'm not," I said. "You can, though."

"Me neither," Steven said, "not with these pain meds." Again, gratitude swept over me.

"Well, I guess just OJ won't hurt. One brunch." He poured himself a glass from the pitcher on the table.

"Hey, guys!" Dinah and Christopher joined us. Dinah gave us both huge hugs. I felt her belly, even if it was way too soon to feel it kick. I would be a good godfather to her child. There was that gratitude again.

"I guess just OJ for you, too, hey, Dinah?" Aaron asked, offering her the pitcher. "You can have a drink drink, though, right, Chris?"

"No, he'll have juice. If I get just juice, he gets just juice."

"This is definitely one of those '*we* are pregnant' things," he said, grinning at my best hag.

"Tell me that when you get morning sickness," she said, playfully slapping his arm.

"Oh God, there better be vodka in that," Brandon said, sliding up to the table. He'd looked better, that's for sure.

"Rough night?" Dinah asked.

"You wouldn't believe it if I told you," he said. "I haven't slept. God, I need a drink."

More gratitude swept over me, that it wasn't me, hung over and hurting and needing that something just to face the day. Steven looked at me and smiled, and I knew he knew what I was thinking. Like he always knew what I was thinking.

He squeezed my knee under the table and I leaned over and kissed him.

"Awwwwwwwww," our friends collectively sighed.

"Well, look who it is," Brandon said. "It's the Wonder Twins. I am amazed to see you guys here this morning."

Jesse and Colton blushed in unison.

"What happened?"

"Oh, just bar shit," Colton said.

"Yeah, nothing important," Jesse said.

Steven's face fell, and I knew what he was thinking. Maybe I was getting the hang of it.

"Look guys, don't worry about me, or about us. We want to know what happened. Believe me, we could use the distraction. Now, tell us."

"Well," Jesse said, with a look at Colton.

"Well," Colton said, with a look at Jesse.

"Oh, for fuck sake, guys," Brandon said. "I'll tell them. So, it started on Thursday. It was just another normal night at Wonderland . . ."

Normal at Wonderland? *Normal* was just a word.

Don't miss where it all began, in *Wonderland*, available now . . .

Boy Meets Boy. Boy Loses Boy.
Boy Goes to Wonderland . . .

After six months of hot-and-heavy dating, Alex is ready to say good-bye to the sex-drugs-and-dance-till-dawn lifestyle and settle down with the love of his life, Steven. He's even bought an engagement ring. But when Steven finds an illicit party favor in Alex's pocket, the powder hits the fan. Steven breaks it off, and Alex heads out to drown his sorrows—in *Wonderland*. . . .

The hottest, hippest nightclub in town, Wonderland is where every boy's dreams come true. Where the DJ, Hatter, spins the maddest tracks, the Caterpillar sells the trippiest drugs, and the Queen of Hearts sends every drag diva off with her head. Still, Alex can't stop thinking about Steven—even while being seduced by a pair of twinks who are tweedlehot and tweedlehotter. Things only get weirder when Alex learns that Steven is missing—and an anonymous phone call warns him that he'll never see Steven again . . . unless he eats this, drinks that, and dives deeper down the rabbit hole of decadence. This certainly isn't just another weekend—in *Wonderland*. . . .

Chapter 1

I looked around the club and couldn't believe no one seemed to care. The party was still going on! In the booth, the Hatter was on the decks, spinning away, without a worry in the world, and below him, on the dance floor, it was a sea of bodies, shirtless, glittered, glistening. Strobes flashed and lasers wove among the crowd, and heads were thrown back, hands in the air, in ecstasy. On Ecstasy, maybe. Who knew? Sure enough, the Caterpillar was at his table, and people visited him briefly, their money for his drugs, and then they were off to the bathroom, to snort, to drop, to bump whatever he'd sold them.

The air vibrated. It was the bass pounding off the dance floor, it was a hundred conversations being yelled out over the din. Here, the twins, in their matching tanks, eyes closed, muscles bulging, as they gyrated together in a cage. There, a flock of mindless twinks, fluttering about in the drama of the moment. Didn't they know? Didn't they care?

I sipped my gin and cran, and shook my head. I wanted to scream! Wanted to grab some passing boy and shake him till he understood. Maybe he'd only mattered to me. Maybe I was the only one who really loved him. Maybe to everyone else, he'd just been a face in the crowd, just one nameless pretty boy among all the other nameless pretty boys.

From the first moment I laid eyes on him though, getting into his white VW Rabbit, he had been so much more to me than just some nameless pretty boy. Sure, right then, he'd just been nameless and pretty, but for the brief second his gaze met mine across the parking lot, we connected. In those few seconds, I imagined a hundred scenarios, and in all of them, we ended up with a white-picket fence, happy-ever-after in Suburbia, away from this sea of smooth bodies, fast beats, and hard drugs.

Away from Wonderland.

But no, now he was gone, and the party was still going, and I was still sitting here, on my perch at the bar, where I sat night in and night out, watching the freak-show train wreck I called my life. And no one in this club could give a shit. Give a bump maybe, or get shittered, but actually care? Actually reach out and genuinely connect with another human being?

Unlikely.

The Hatter spun, and the Caterpillar sold, and the people danced, and I sat there, staring at my ice cubes, thinking it was time to go home, knowing I would order one more. It was a Friday night, and that's what I did. What we all did. We left our real world, our nine-to-fives, our condos in the sky, and we came down here, under the traffic, to a dirty little hole that lit up with beautiful lights, and even more beautiful people.

"Another?"

It was Brandon, beautiful and blond, all abs to the front, all amazing ass to the rear, and he was leaning across the bar. His eyes were blue, and my drink was empty.

"Sure." His fingers brushed the back of my hand as he took away my empty, replaced it with another.

"On me," he said, and he was back to the lineup. I watched him for a while, doing the graceful dance of the bartender. He spun about, pouring shots, cracking beers, dispensing drinks and flirts and seven-dollar ounces of happiness.

I twirled the drink around in my hands. I really had had enough, and I knew I should go, but I hoped he'd come. Still. Even though the Hatter had already announced last call for the first time. Even though the last thing Steven had said to me was that he never wanted to see me again. He couldn't have meant it though. It was the heat of the moment and when he calmed down, when we both calmed down, we'd work it out. He'd come down those stairs, and through the crowd, and he'd take me by the hand and lead me to the dance floor, and with our bodies pressed together, we would kiss under the strobe, like we did that first night, and everything would be the way it was.

"You have five minutes left until last call," the Hatter counted down on the mic, and Kesha mixed with One Direction, and the twinks squealed and the dance floor, already full, bulged with more people, one big writhing mass of beautiful, tragic homos. And not one of them knew or cared that he was gone, and it was over, and my drink was empty again.

"Brandon!" I yelled as he spun past me, dropping drinks down at the other end of the bar.

"Another?"

"Make it two," I said, and slid a twenty toward him. He dropped off the drinks and my change, and I took the drinks, left the change. It was just money. And his ass was easily worth the tip.

I pushed back my stool, lurched to my feet, drink in each hand, and fought my way through the crowd. Eyes went up and down me, in that judging homo way. My eyes went up and down the people I passed, just as judging. I wove my way through fat straight girls and their skinny gay best friends, past the plaid-wearing lesbians playing pool in the corner, my eyes on the Caterpillar. I knew I shouldn't. I knew Steven wouldn't like it.

But he hadn't come. And if all these people didn't care, why should I?

"Alex!" I heard my name as an arm wrapped around my waist. An arm attached to the gleaming torso of one of the twins. He pulled me into him, and I lifted my drinks over his shoulders as we hugged, as we kissed each other's cheeks. "How's your night?"

"It's a night," I said, sipping my drink, my eyes darting past whichever twin this was to the table in the corner, where the Caterpillar watched and waited. "Yours?"

"Where's Steven?"

There it was. His name. Hearing it made my chest tighten. "He didn't come out tonight."

"Too bad! Come dance with us!" He went to take me by the hand as his look-alike came up and grabbed me by the other. I felt my drink spill down my arm.

"No, I was just headed home. I—"

"One dance?" Two matching smiles, four matching dimples, four sparkling green eyes, so much muscle. How could I say no? And with Steven not here, why should I say no?

And then we were on the dance floor, hands in the air, and I had one in front of me, grinding back into my crotch, and one behind me, grinding into my butt, and all around me, people danced and laughed and drank, and the lights were bright, and the music was wordless and fast, and faster and faster we danced, and I finished my drinks and threw back my head, and let myself get lost in the moment.

Steven hadn't come. I had waited and waited and waited, and he hadn't come. He had made his choice. The twin behind me was kissing my neck. I tilted my head back and met his lips with mine. He tasted like berries.

I twisted around so we were facing each other. Behind me, the other one lifted up my shirt, and I let him take it off. His lips were on my shoulders, and I paused briefly, thinking how I must look between their tanned and toned bodies. But then the one behind me slid a hand into my pants and I stopped thinking. And we danced and we kissed, sweat and skin and sweet sweet sin.

In the mirror that ran along the dance floor, I saw us, and what a sight we were, the three of us, three among the many, and it was wonderful and it was beautiful and it was wrong. It wasn't Steven. And there, at the end of the mirror, I could see the Caterpillar's reflection, as he sat there, beer in hand, and watched and waited.

Waited for me?

I squirmed out from between the twins, and their hands followed mine until the crowd separated us, and I looked back at them. Their hands had found each other, and they were kissing, and people watched as they danced, because the twins were beautiful and shirtless and gleaming, looking enough like actual brothers to be forbidden, taboo, exciting. I wound my way across the floor and up the stairs, and sat down across from the Caterpillar.

He smiled at me, raised his beer in salute. I raised an eyebrow in question, and I could feel the desperation on my face. It was late. What if he was out? He nodded, and I could feel the relief and the guilt and the excitement all mingle inside me. I slid my hand across the table, money hidden in my palm. He shook my hand, and I could feel the money disappear, feel the familiar little plastic Baggie.

Away from the Caterpillar I went, and back through the throng, now even more frenzied as the Hatter announced, "Last song of the night." People were flooding onto the dance floor, and I was going against the stream, headed to the bathroom, where the strobes and lasers and swirling color went away, in an ugly fluorescent glare. I locked the stall behind me, ignoring the water all over the floor, the clumped toilet paper, the unflushed bowl.

I held up the Baggie, flicked it to loosen it, opened it up. I dipped in my key, scooped out some powder, and inhaled. My body tensed and then loosened. I was floating on fire.

Tucking the Baggie into my jeans, I checked my reflection in the mirror, looking for any telltale signs of drug use. Finding none, and not really caring either way, I went back out in the club, where everything seemed more real now. The music was just a little clearer, the lights were just a tad brighter. The twins were still lip-locked on the dance floor. I fought my way toward them, and reached them just as the song faded away into the silence of a hundred conversations, laughter and shrieks and disjointed words.

I was high and alive, and I had a twin on each side, and as the three of us found our way out of Wonderland and into the world above, I looked around the club one last time, and right then, I didn't care either.

Chasing rabbits can lead to danger...

WONDERLAND

A NOVEL

ROB BROWATZKE

About the Author

Rob Browatzke has been writing for as long as he can remember, and is pretty darn excited for someone else to be reading his stuff finally! When it comes to gay bars and booze and drugs and drama, he knows what he's talking about. He has over fifteen years of experience working in gay clubs in Edmonton, Alberta, and his current Wonder-lounge is every bit as amazing as Alex's Wonderland. Feel free to stalk him on Facebook and Twitter @robbrowatzke.

Printed in the United States
by Baker & Taylor Publisher Services